"Seriously?" His deep voice entered the room before he even walked in. **"I do not need a PR strategist."**

"A liaison aide, sir," his aide murmured.

Beatrice stood as she'd been instructed earlier, but as he entered, every assumption she'd made about him was wiped away.

Prince Julius brimmed, not just with authority but with health and energy. It was as if a force field had entered the room.

She had dealt with alpha males and females at the top of their game—or rather, usually when they were crashing from the top.

Not he.

He was, quite literally, stunning.

He stunned.

"It's a pleasure to meet you," she said and then added, "sir."

"Likewise," he said, even if his eyes said otherwise.

God, he was tall, Beatrice thought. But it was more than just his height—he was the most immaculate man she had ever seen.

Beatrice swallowed, not wanting to pursue that line of thought. The issue was that at most interviews she had found people were less in the flesh.

He was so, so much more.

Carol Marinelli recently filled in a form asking for her job title. Thrilled to be able to put down her answer, she put "writer." Then it asked what Carol did for relaxation and she put down the truth—"writing." The third question asked for her hobbies. Well, not wanting to look obsessed, she crossed her fingers and answered "swimming"—but, given that the chlorine in the pool does terrible things to her highlights, I'm sure you can guess the real answer!

Carol Marinelli

INNOCENT UNTIL HIS FORBIDDEN TOUCH

HARLEQUIN

PRESENTS

Recycling programs for this product may not exist in your area.

ISBN-13: 978-1-335-73866-0

Innocent Until His Forbidden Touch

Copyright © 2022 by Carol Marinelli

Harlequin Enterprises ULC
22 Adelaide St. West, 41st Floor
Toronto, Ontario M5H 4E3, Canada
www.Harlequin.com

Printed in U.S.A.

INNOCENT UNTIL HIS FORBIDDEN TOUCH

PROLOGUE

Ten years ago...

BEATRICE DID NOT arrive at the convent unannounced.

It had taken her a long time, not only to save the airfare from London, but to receive a response to her repeated requests to meet with the Reverend Mother. She had been told her journey was unnecessary and that there was nothing more she could be told regarding her circumstances...

As she walked up the hill for her midday interview, Beatrice consoled herself with the fact that even if there was nothing more to glean about her mother then she would find out about her dear friend.

They had been abandoned three weeks apart and had been as different as two babies—and later two children—could be.

Alicia, dark and vibrant; Beatrice her pale, timid shadow.

They had been such unlikely friends. Yet, for whatever reason, Alicia had taken a battering ram to her heart and insisted they were better than friends—more than sisters, even. In fact, she'd often declared, they were twins!

Aged eleven, Beatrice had been awarded a scholarship and sent to an esteemed boarding school in Milan. Beatrice had shivered in terror, but Alicia had tried to be brave, and they had sworn to stay in touch. Alicia had even told her to work hard and get a good job so they could be flat-mates someday.

It had been a glimpse of the future that Beatrice had held on to. The scariest part of being abandoned had always been the thought of what might come after they left the convent gates—but they would have each other.

Alicia had barely been able to read, certainly hadn't been able to write, but it hadn't deterred Beatrice—she had written regularly. And then, just as she'd got her bearings in Milan, she'd been sent to a small abbey in Switzerland for language immersion. There had been no other children and certainly no teenagers or any chance of making friends there. The order had been strict, but occasionally she'd be granted permission to call the convent in Trebordi. To no avail. They'd never brought Alicia to the phone, saying she was in prayers, or with friends, or in detention.

Any excuse.

Alicia had always tended towards melodrama, and Beatrice had guessed they didn't want to deal with the upset her phone calls might cause. She'd begun to wonder if Alicia had even received her letters, and had vowed to return in person as soon as she could afford to do so.

Her final two years of school had been in England, where she'd been labelled standoffish rather than shy. Aloof. Cold.

It had been the same in her first year of university...

While her English was excellent, in those first getting-to-know-you exchanges Beatrice had always remained a beat behind. Her sense of humour had been lacking, and sarcasm truly wasted on her—by the time she'd worked out that people were joking it was too late.

She hadn't been able to get past even the first questions— *Where are you from...? What do your family do...?*

She walked on and lingered at the baby door, where she

had been left as a newborn some nineteen years ago. She thought of her mother's fear and loneliness. She too had grown up feeling exactly that.

Scared.

Lonely.

She'd had Alicia though, Beatrice reminded herself.

Having rung the bell at the gates, she smiled, a little bemused, when it was Reverend Mother herself who came to let her in.

'I'm so excited to be back…' Her words, for once, tumbled out. Beatrice felt the heat on her cheeks and the glow in her heart as she walked the familiar path to the convent.

'What time is your train?' Reverend Mother asked, walking briskly. 'You are going back to England tonight, yes?'

'Oh, no, I'm planning to stay in Trebordi for a week or two,' Beatrice replied, hoping Reverend Mother might extend an invitation.

As they climbed the stairs to her office, Beatrice found out that was not to be.

'We cannot have all the children we've ever cared for using the place as a hostel…' She was terse, but softened it with a smile. 'I have to be like a cat,' she explained. 'I am kind to the kittens, but soon it is time to stand back and allow them independence—force it at times.'

'I *am* independent, Reverend Mother.'

'You are on a full scholarship at university?'

'I am.' Beatrice felt a little insulted, but was unable to show it. While grateful for the scholarship, she had worked hard for it. Still worked hard. She'd found a job at a chemist's in England, and now… 'I work as a translator in a hospital in the evenings and at weekends.'

She took a seat in Reverend Mother's office, keeping her smile in place and taking out her notebook and pen.

'Child, you can put those away. There is nothing more I can tell you.'

'Perhaps…' Beatrice held firm. 'But I remember that Alicia had gold earrings pinned to her baby suit. *Segni di ricooscimento*. Signs of recognition. I have read that should a mother return she can identify her child that way.'

'Beatrice, I have told you. For you there was nothing.'

'There must have been something,' she replied. 'A page of the bible…?' She had been told her mother was presumed to have been a tourist, attending the festival that came to Trebordi each year—especially given that Beatrice was so blonde. 'Perhaps a trinket from the festival.'

'Beatrice, if there was anything I would have told you.'

'A nappy?' she asked, tears stinging her eyes, embarrassed at the thought that she had been left uncovered and naked. Discarded. 'Something?'

'This doesn't help anyone,' Reverend Mother scolded. 'Beatrice, you have had an education most people could only dream of. Let it go.'

'No,' Beatrice said. 'I won't. I worry for my mother. If something dreadful happened to her, then I want her to know I understand. And if she was young and scared, I want to tell her myself that I know how it feels to be scared and alone. I love her, and so of course I forgive her.'

'It's not healthy, Beatrice. I have seen many children devote too much time trying so hard to get to the past that they ruin their future.'

'Well, I want to know my history. I will stand at the baby door every year, and I will be here each year for Alicia's birthday too…' She saw the flush on Reverend Mother's cheeks, and it was there in that office that Beatrice learned how to be direct. Although she was usually timid, she found out just how tough she could be. 'Did Alicia even get my letters?'

'Of course.'

Reverend Mother wouldn't lie, surely?

Only Beatrice felt sure that she was, and her pale blue eyes narrowed in suspicion as she was repeatedly stone-walled.

It took everything she could summon for her to confront the Reverend Mother. 'I don't believe she did.'

'Please show the respect you were taught.'

'Reverend Mother, I respectfully ask you, where is my friend?'

Reverend Mother responded with silence.

'Well, if you won't tell me, I'm going to ask around the village. I have enough money to stay at the bar.' *Barely.* 'I might go and visit Signora Schininà.' She was the woman who ran the brothel. 'She knows all the gossip, and her son was close to Alicia...'

'She's dead.'

'Well, I'll just ask someone else, and I'll keep asking—'

'Child...' Reverend Mother interjected. '*Non destare il cane che dorme.* Do not awaken the sleeping dog.'

What sleeping dog?

Why did her very presence seem to cause such unease?

Surely foundlings returned here all the time in search of their history?

'I'm not leaving Trebordi until I have answers.' She closed her notebook and put her pen in her bag, sat aloof and defiant even as her heart pounded in her chest. 'I will go to every shop, knock on every door...'

Reverend Mother stood, clearly flustered. 'Please wait.'

Beatrice sat for what felt like an age. She waited an hour, perhaps two, for Reverend Mother to return. Eventually she stood up and went to the window, staring not at the ocean but at the playground of the little school she'd attended. Alicia would clamber on top of the climbing frame to wave to her friend Dante as he boarded the bus to the school in the village. They'd been ten! Then her loud companion would round up a group of girls and play complicated games while Beatrice resisted.

Despite the happy promise of her name, she'd been a guarded child, who had loathed playtime and dreaded the bell and the scrape of chairs as the girls raced out. Serious and prim by nature, she had felt too old for games even at five, preferring to sit by the water taps, simply not knowing how to join in.

Alicia, though, had been so bold, confident and sunny. She'd happily peel off her dress to swim in her knickers in the river, and had held hands with boys in the village—well, with one. There'd been no swimming in the river for Beatrice. She would emerge from the bathroom fully dressed each morning and undress in there each night, always so private and shy...

It vexed her that she'd been left naked. Exposed.

Beatrice turned as the office door opened—but not to show the round, familiar face of Reverend Mother.

'Sister Catherine.' Beatrice gave her a tight smile, assuming she was here to explain the delay, or offer refreshments, perhaps.

'I have been told you have questions.' Sister Catherine gestured for her to sit.

'Many,' Beatrice said. 'Were you here when I was found?'

Sister Catherine was a very nondescript woman—not just in looks, but in the bank of Beatrice's memory. Dark hair peeked from her habit and dark brows arched over brown eyes. She'd been a little mean, but not dreadfully so. More...indifferent. She had taught Latin, and Beatrice had been the star of that class, but on her own merit.

Sister Catherine hadn't been particularly encouraging. Just... Nothing.

And then Beatrice found out that she was her mother.

'I was plain, like you,' she said, 'and cheerless too.'

Beatrice said nothing, just stared at the features that were, she could now see, a dark version of her own. How had she never seen it? How had her own mother been in plain sight and she hadn't known?

'I did have one curiosity, though…'

Nothing dreadful had happened to her. It had been nothing but a curiosity she'd wished to satisfy before committing to the church.

'I used to help my mother clean the cottages where the tourists stayed. He was a widower. He had been married for thirty years and he missed his wife dreadfully. He was here from Germany for a quiet vacation.'

'So he wasn't here for the festival?'

'No!' Sister Catherine scorned the very thought. 'He was a historian—and he liked to live in the past too. He said I reminded him of his late wife when she was young.'

'He took advantage?'

'No, I was twenty-five and he was handsome indeed.'

Beatrice's past was being given to her rather like a history lesson—with little emotion, just a small summing-up. Two weeks of sin and then she'd repented.

'I was a novice when I realised I was with child, and…'

'Scared?'

It would seem not.

'Beatrice, I knew what I wanted to do with my life, and I knew that you would be taken care of…'

'Did Reverend Mother know?'

'Of course not,' she said rather harshly, and it was that part that shrivelled Beatrice's heart.

Reverend Mother noticed *everything*. Nothing got past her. And yet Sister Catherine's pregnancy somehow had.

Beatrice's very birth somehow had. Clearly she had not done anything to alert Reverend Mother.

'It was when you turned ten, or around then, that Reverend Mother called me in here. She said the similarities were striking and could no longer be ignored. In truth, I couldn't see it. We are both petite, but you are so blonde...'

How could she not have seen it? For now Beatrice felt as if she were looking in a mirror. Or at one of those apps that aged you, but not much...just a little. It showed her what she'd look like with dark hair and dark eyes...

She searched for a memory of them both—a stolen moment, an extra treat, a bedtime story... Finally she found one—only it wasn't endearing.

One day the bell had gone for the dreaded playtime and she'd pleaded to stay in and read quietly.

'Andate a giocare fuori.' Sister Catherine hadn't even looked up.

Go and play outside.

Beatrice's voice, when it came, was hoarse. 'I used to climb out of the window and go to the festival, searching for you.' Then she would wake screaming and wet and she and Alicia would sneak down to the laundry to wash the sheets. 'I used to go every night when the festival was in town.'

'The festival has gone now,' Sister Catherine said. 'And so has your friend.'

'Where?'

'I don't know.' Sister Catherine shrugged. 'You have your answers. I have been honest...' She spread her hands, as if asking what more she could want. 'There's nothing for you here—just trouble for me if you stay. Beatrice, you have been fed and cared for, given an education I could never have afforded...'

But not loved.

Not for a single second.

Instead, she had been hidden in plain sight, and then when it had become inconvenient, she had been moved on.

'You didn't wrap me... You didn't cover me...'

'I knew you'd be found.'

Beatrice discovered sarcasm then. 'How caring of you.'

She left and took a local taxi to the train station, vowing never, ever to return. So appalled was she by the answers she'd found, she gave up on finding Alicia too. Instead, she sat on the train and cut her mother from the one photo of the convent inhabitants she had from her childhood, and then she decided to change her surname from Festa to Taylor.

Cut, cut, cut.

She snipped her mother into tiny pieces and refused to shed so much as a single tear.

Beatrice knew then why she was so emotionally frozen. She hadn't developed a heart of stone, she realised. Rather, she'd inherited one!

And now Beatrice Taylor would use it to her own advantage.

CHAPTER ONE

'*SIGNORA, ALLACCI LA cintura di sicurezza*. Fasten your seat-belt.'

The captain apologised for the rough air that had accompanied them, and the storm cells that had meant their flight path had taken them over Sicily.

Bellanisiá was, Beatrice decided as they commenced their descent, just a little too close to Trebordi for comfort. And she wasn't sure she even wanted the job.

Liaison Aide to HRH Prince Julius of Bellanisiá.

It was a newly created role for a newly appointed heir.

The brief was simple: tidy up the reprobate Prince's image prior to bridal selection.

Her career was PR. She cleaned up the images of fallen celebrities, MPs, sportsmen, or whoever needed her detached aloofness to help them navigate whatever mess they'd found themselves in. Affairs, dramas and lies—Beatrice just waded her emotionless way through it all. No one would guess that the brittle woman who could face press or cameras and address sensitive topics with ease had never so much as been kissed. Or that she'd struggled to make a single friend.

She worked on three- to six-month contracts and was successful enough to be approached for work through word of mouth rather than having to seek it out.

The secret to her success? Beatrice didn't care. And she told all her clients just that—she wasn't their agent, nor their wife, mother, psychologist…

While a royal wedding was an attractive enough incentive to have sustained her through three panel interviews, Beatrice herself now had doubts that she was suited to the role.

Deference was not on her impressive list of attributes. And, judging by the lengthy list of protocols she'd been forwarded just to meet with the arrogant Prince, deference was a prerequisite.

It was *his* life that was in chaos, Beatrice would politely remind him, not hers.

Their flight path, though unsettling, had offered an enticing view of the Kingdom of Bellanisiá. A beautiful archipelago of islands in the Ionian Sea, it looked from the sky as if pebbles had been skimmed between Sicily and Greece. Each island was unique, but all existed under one rule.

In preparation for her first interview Beatrice had done some research online, and had caught up with Prince Julius's life.

A wild child…

A surprisingly happy teen compared to his very formal elder brother and elder sister…

And as an adult…?

He'd studied archaeology, followed by a stint in the military, and should now have an honorary PhD in brunettes—tall brunettes, widowed brunettes, curvy brunettes—all beautiful, all devoted. He had looks, charm, and all the benefits of being second in line to the throne.

Hetaerae were allowed—basically long-term trusted mistresses—as well as a wife, but Julius selected his own short-term company on his extensive travels.

Sitting in her temporary flat in London, about to finish her latest temporary job, Beatrice had topped up her hot water and lemon and read all she could on the maverick Prince.

He disappeared for months on end on archaeological excavations, then returned for duty and to party. His life, though, had swerved out of the fast lane and careered into the emergency one when his elder brother Prince Claude had died, suddenly and unexpectedly, a year ago from flu.

Prince Julius had returned to reside at the palace, where not only had his passion for archaeology been put aside, but his short-term relationships had halted and become... well, not relationships. All his flings now seemed to be with exes.

There was nothing tawdry—just gossip. He partied hard; he worked harder. From all she could glean, Prince Julius had not only taken on the role and responsibilities of his late brother, but the Queen had also retreated from duties, and he was picking up the slack.

Even after three interviews, she knew little more than the fact that the palace wanted to curb his ways and plan his wedding.

Beatrice had had several questions of her own. 'He's opposed to women in the line of succession?' she'd asked at the third interview.

Beatrice had felt her chin meet her neck and her mouth gape at the cheek of that when she'd first read it, but the tone of her enquiry had been polite.

'That's not your concern,' Phillipe, Head of Palace Protocol, had informed her.

'Actually, it is—if I'm trying to update his image.'

'That changes with the next generation,' Jordan, the Prince's PA, had responded. 'Things move slowly here.'

Indeed, it seemed they did. So slowly that when Beatrice

arrived at her hotel, the receptionist informed her that the dresses she needed pressing wouldn't be returned until later that night.

'I have a meeting at the palace at two,' Beatrice said in swift Italian. 'I would like it taken care of now, please. Thank you.'

After a quick shower, she clipped her blonde hair back, put on a slick of pale lipstick, and topped her crisply pressed grey shift dress with a darker grey jacket for a neutral look.

Neutral.

When she'd been a translator, her aim had been not to draw the eye. Now, given the status of most of her clients, her aim remained the same.

A car collected her, and on arrival at the rear of the palace there was a rigorous checking of her bag and pockets, and her phone was retained.

Then she was given another tutorial on protocol, and also informed, at a pre meeting the Prince meeting, that her car today was an exception and there was a shuttle bus for most palace staff.

Beatrice had by then decided she did not want the job.

She was led down a glass passageway to a very plush office and told that, should she get the role, her own office would be two floors down.

Of course.

She awaited this unsuitable heir who was being prepared for the altar.

Beatrice already knew he was handsome, but she was expecting him to be…well, *petulant*, as well as wrung out from the effort of balancing his workload with his rather decadent ways.

He was fully thirty minutes late.

'Seriously?' His deep voice carried ahead of him,

speaking in Italian, and then he walked in. 'I do not need a PR strategist.'

'A liaison aide, sir,' his companion murmured.

Beatrice stood, as she'd been instructed to do, but when he entered the room every assumption she'd had was wiped out.

Prince Julius brimmed not just with authority but with health and energy. It was as if some force field had entered the room.

She dealt with alphas both male and female at the top of their game—or rather, when they were about to come crashing down from it.

Not he.

He was, quite literally, stunning.

He stunned.

So much so that although the main language here was Italian, followed by Greek, Beatrice spoke in English, the language she'd last been working in from the country she had flown in from.

'It's a pleasure to meet you,' she said, and then added, because she'd been told to do so, 'sir.'

'Likewise,' he said, though his eyes said otherwise.

In truth, he'd discarded her on sight. Certainly he had not registered her features.

No doubt, like so many, he had just briefly surmised that the petite blonde in her smart grey shift dress did not have what was required to deal with the intricate details of his complex life.

God, he's tall, Beatrice thought, almost relieved when he gestured for her to take a seat.

It was more than his height—he was the most immaculate man she had ever seen. His hair was black and glossy and cut to perfection. His silver-grey tie was knotted and perfectly so. From his citrussy scent and manicured nails to his porcelain-capped teeth and black eyes, he looked as if he'd just stepped off a magazine cover, or a director had shouted *Cut!* while shooting a film about—

Beatrice swallowed. She did not want to pursue that line of thought. The issue was that at most interviews she found so-called alphas to be much less in the flesh.

He was so much more.

Just too good-looking.

The unrufflable Beatrice put the flutter in her chest down to nerves.

He was royal; it must be that.

Staff were standing to either side of him, and he'd frowned as he read the bullet points of her résumé. 'Sicilian?'

'*Si, tuttavia—*' Beatrice responded in Italian but he halted her.

'Let's stay in English,' he suggested. 'I need the practice; mine is a little rusty.'

He glanced again at her résumé, presumably at her list of rather impressive clients, and then looked up at his PA, Jordan, whom, like the others, Beatrice had met at the interviews.

'No.' He shook his head. 'I really don't want my name attached to any of these people…' His top lip curled a little.

'Sir…' Jordan nodded in understanding. 'Ms Taylor is here more to assist with the press interest and your image in the lead-up to bridal selection.'

'I agreed to a reset.' The Prince turned his head and glared up to a man Beatrice knew to be one of the King's aides. 'Not to being policed.'

'I certainly won't police anyone,' Beatrice interjected. 'Sir.'

Everyone stiffened when she spoke uninvited. Well, all apart from the Prince. He glanced up, and those black eyes met hers for the first time. She put the flutter in her chest down to butterflies.

With the wings of bats.

'You studied Classical and Modern Languages...' He frowned at the details of her career path and mentioned one of the embassies she had worked in. 'You worked as a translator there?'

'Yes, sir.'

His lips pursed a fraction. Possibly he was recalling a scandal around that time that had shifted the course of her work.

'You were a hospital and then a court translator prior to that?'

'There should be a reference there, concerning my clear and accurate translations.' Somebody coughed, and Beatrice realised her omission and added, 'Sir.'

Gosh, how was she supposed to discuss scandals and such if she had to bow and address him so formally at all times? While she *wanted* a royal wedding on her résumé, in order for her to do her work well there would need to be a lot of straight talking involved.

He rested his hand on his chin and pressed a finger to his lips as he read the brief pages her lengthy résumé had been condensed down to for his perusal.

'I think this might be an issue.' He looked up at an advisor. 'If Ms Taylor translated at this embassy...'

'I have to agree, sir,' said Phillipe. 'I've made my objections clear.'

There were...political issues between our countries.

It was Beatrice who answered. 'They are more than happy to provide further references. They know I won't be a fly on anyone's wall, sir.'

Again, he met her eyes.

Beatrice held them.

'Do you have any questions for me?' he asked.

'Several.' Beatrice nodded. 'The first being how frank am I allowed to be, sir?'

'Allowed?' His eyes narrowed at the implication.

'For example, if I took the role would we be able to speak one to one?' Beatrice asked.

'Of course,' Prince Julius responded. 'In fact let's do so now.'

Beatrice wasn't sure if she was nervous as she stood up, for she so rarely was. Yet her heart was beating faster in her chest, as if she were climbing stairs rather than descending them. French doors were being opened by a servant, and she felt an unfamiliar hesitancy before stepping outside.

He was a prince, Beatrice reminded herself. A prince she was about to confront. It was natural to feel nervous. However, nervous felt like the wrong choice of word.

It should be a relief to step outside after the rather hostile atmosphere indoors, yet her tension felt heightened out in the soft afternoon breeze and in surroundings so tranquil they should calm her.

'I apologise for the tension back there,' he said. 'You would be the first member of the palace team who is not from Bellanisiá.'

'I see.'

'There are centuries of tradition here—ancient laws from many cultures, many languages spoken. I assume you already know that?'

'I've read as much as I can of the kingdom's history.'

'Then you will also know that I've enjoyed the bachelor life. However, given I am now heir to the throne, it's time for the leopard to change his spots.'

He wasn't a leopard.

Nor a cheetah.

Not even a growling lion.

It was like walking beside a giant black panther and being told by his gushing owners that he was completely tame.

Nor was he cute—and he certainly wasn't particularly friendly.

'The lake is beautiful,' Beatrice said, unusually tentative in her approach. 'It's like winter...'

'Lago Lefko,' he said.

White Lake, Beatrice thought. A mixture of Greek and Italian. She could see why it had been named as such.

It was surrounded by white willows, silver birch, even the stones around it were white, and glinted as if covered in frost. It even felt as if the temperature had dropped and she shivered slightly.

'I almost expect my breath to blow white. Even the birds...' There were doves in the trees and Japanese cranes on a central island.

'The doves were introduced when my parents married.' He pointed to the cranes, making hearts with their necks. 'They were a gift when Prince Claude was born, and the white swans were for Princess Jasmine.'

'And you?'

'I beg your pardon?'

'Were birds introduced when you...?' She suddenly realised that he had perfectly understood what she had said. 'Sir.'

'Peacocks,' he told her. 'White, of course.'

Beatrice looked around.

'They're always off preening. You will soon hear them.'

He spoke politely, yet he was removed and distant. There was a wall between them that she doubted would be dismantled even on commencement of her job, for she had seen how formal his staff were.

'So, you have questions?'

'Yes. It was the one-year anniversary of Prince Claude's passing last week.'

'Indeed.'

'And from my understanding it is now considered time for the country to look towards happier times.' She trod gently, out of politeness and also because it was beyond anything she knew, but she did try to put her client first. 'Is marriage something you want?'

'It's necessary.'

'I understand that, but I'm trying to gauge your thoughts and—'

'You won't get my thoughts, Ms Taylor. Are you always this direct?'

'I am.' She was. 'And I don't see how we can have the conversations it will be necessary for us to have if I have to constantly bow and call you *sir*…sir.'

'That's your issue to deal with,' he told her. 'I prefer to keep things formal.'

He was awful, Beatrice decided.

'I *will* tell you that my future wife will have her own country's interests at hand when she makes her decision to marry me. It will be a very mutually beneficial partnership and it will be celebrated.'

'And love?'

He managed a wry laugh at that. 'I don't need that sort of complication.' He turned his head to her. 'Would you bring *your* partner to work?'

Beatrice had never had a partner, and even though she might be delving into his private life the Prince wouldn't be getting a whiff of hers. 'Of course not.'

'Or to a business dinner? Or on a business trip?'

'No.'

'Precisely.'

'I don't sleep with my colleagues, though,' Beatrice added. 'Or have their children.'

'You're a commoner, Ms Taylor. I am not.'

She could have cheerfully pushed him into that lake. She doubted she'd be offered the job now, let alone take it.

'There was an incident a few weeks ago…' Beatrice chose the latest example. 'And an apology issued by the palace.'

'How would you have dealt with it?' asked the Prince.

'From everything I've read, it seems that a good time was had by all.' She sounded tough. And liberated, even. Which she was. Just not on a private level. It was much easier to discuss other people's wild ways when they were so alien to her own. 'I didn't see your need to comment.'

'I didn't.'

'Well, the palace did,' Beatrice pointed out. 'There have been denials and apologies as far back as I can see. On your behalf, of course.' She glanced over at him, and then upwards; he really was very tall. 'It's not how I'd have played it.'

'It's not a game, Ms Taylor. And, yet again, you are to address me as *sir*.'

'Of course.' She gave a tight smile. 'I'm just trying to get a clearer picture, sir.'

'Well, currently I seem to be being portrayed as some sort of prodigal son returning—though without the celebration.'

'By whom?'

He stared ahead.

'The palace? The King?' she probed.

He didn't respond directly. 'I make no apologies—however, they continually do. On my behalf. The press also drags stuff up, hoping if they push…' He gave a tight shrug. 'It is not the best way to go into a marriage.'

Normally her clients were pleading with her to fix their problems, but not him.

'Well, if you're to spare the embarrassed blushes of your future bride it would help if things were toned down. Your lovers seem to adore you,' Beatrice said. 'There's no specific scandal, as such. Just… You spread your affections generously, sir.'

'There hasn't been a lot of affection,' he admitted. 'Not this past year. But my—' He halted; it was clear Prince Julius did not discuss his private life with anyone. Even the woman who might be hired to shine it up. 'I've agreed to lie low for a couple of months prior to signing the Document of Intent.'

'Well, that's a start. But the palace, in my opinion, has to stop apologising and issuing statements. If I got the job, everything would have to go through me…'

It wasn't out of forgetfulness that she failed to add *sir*— more that a family of black swans were passing. They stood out against all the other birds in and around the lake which were white. The proud parents had six grey signets behind them, with one more peeking out beneath the mother's wings. They were so cute that if she hadn't been at an interview Beatrice might have rummaged in her bag for a cereal bar to feed them.

The Prince looked at the source of her distraction. 'The two black swans were introduced when Prince Claude passed away.'

'That cygnet is too big to still be on its mother's back…' Beatrice couldn't help but smile as the cygnet turned its head as they sailed past. 'Cute, though.'

'You like birds?' asked Prince Julius, and resumed walking.

'I do,' Beatrice admitted.

'Actually, I have a question.'

'Of course.'

'Does it bother you?' he asked. 'Saying something one day, then being proved a liar the next.'

Beatrice paused, unsure if he was probing her about her latest client, who had rather scandalously been caught cheating *again*, but his question had been casual and she could only hear the note of curiosity to his tone. Still, for the sake of confidentiality she kept her answer a mixture of vague and truthful. 'It doesn't bother me.'

'No?'

'They're not my lies, sir.'

'True.'

'As well as that, I don't…' She was about to give him the spiel she often gave to clients, but refrained. Probably, Beatrice told herself, because he was royal.

'Please…' he invited.

It was an odd moment. The low glare of the morning sun over the white lake gave the appearance of an icy winter, and yet the peacocks were calling as he had said they would. Screeching unseen.

'Go on,' he said, prompting her with her own words. 'As well as that…?'

Very well, then. Beatrice stopped walking and so did he. She stared up at him. 'On a professional level I'm involved, and I do my best, but on a personal level…'

His eyes narrowed more in anticipation than in question, waiting for her to elaborate.

'I don't take things personally.'

He frowned.

'I'm objective. I'm not…' She took a breath and told him what she told all her clients. 'I don't care what you get up to.'

It sounded harsh, yet it was the reason Beatrice was so good at her job. And the reason for her utter detachment?

Well, that was not for potential employers to know. It was not for anyone to know.

Beatrice was close to no one.

'Well,' Prince Julius said, 'that makes a refreshing change.'

To her surprise, she was offered the role.

So Beatrice left London to take on the three-month position in Bellanisiá and signed a lease on a furnished second floor flat there, with a small balcony that looked over the marina.

In her first month there she started to take her evening meal on the balcony, looking out at the expensive yachts and sailing boats, as well as the fishing boats. Cannons were often fired, as if at random, which made her smile. In her second month Beatrice bought a bird feeder, and found herself taking breakfast out there too.

She was growing fond of the place.

Working at the palace was incredible—and not only that, Beatrice found she actually enjoyed taking the shuttle bus to and from work. On her way she always sat to the left, because the views were incredible there, and on her return to the right.

The locals didn't seem to care which side they sat on— they were, of course, more used to the views—and they carried on chatting, or reading, or dozing as the shuttle bus inched its way through the town, picking up palace staff.

There was an all-encompassing mix of designer shops and bazaars and famous fashion houses, as well as florists and bookstores and a gorgeous central square, with government buildings, monuments and houses of worship.

The job was interesting in itself, for there was a lot of pressure from within for the Prince to make haste and marry. A lot of Beatrice's time was spent going head-to-head with his aides, and even with his own team—who were, to her mind, too keen to please the King.

The simple brief to tidy up his image in preparation for marriage, was not so easily executed.

Now, with three weeks to go on her contract, the slurs in the press kept coming, and Prince Julius appeared no closer to signing the Document of Intent, than he had at the commencement of her work.

And Beatrice had found herself dealing with a very unfamiliar issue.

She liked her boss.

Or rather, she had her first ever crush.

And very inconveniently it was on HRH Prince Julius of Bellanisiá!

There had been signs, for those bats had remained in her chest, and sometimes when she met his eyes it felt as if those peacocks were screeching unseen, but she'd simply ignored her unsettled feelings. But taking the shuttle bus to work one morning, as they'd approached the square, she had found her eyes drawn to the stunning central church, with its glorious dome and endless steps.

It was where the royal wedding would take place...

Where Prince Julius would marry.

Her lips had pressed together and a surge of hurt, or perhaps covetousness, had risen in her chest as it had dawned on her that the bats residing there were actually wings of forbidden desire.

Beatrice had hurriedly looked away from the church, but the feeling had not abated.

Instead it had remained.

More accurately, it had grown.

It was so unexpected.

So unfamiliar that she would have done anything to speak with a friend.

It was so disquieting that on her birthday she returned to the place where she'd been born—hoping for what, Beatrice didn't quite know.

Trebordi hadn't changed much in a decade.

Standing on the headland, she held on to her straw hat to stop it from flying away. Until that moment, Beatrice had thought she'd changed. She had changed her surname, her identity, built a career, conversed mainly in English... yet deep down, Beatrice knew she hadn't changed at all.

Here she stood, on her twenty-ninth birthday, staring at the convent in which she'd been raised and she was still as scared and as lonely as the little girl who had grown up there.

More so, even.

She'd had Alicia then.

And now she was more desperate than ever to find her.

Beatrice yearned for advice from her friend. But she didn't know where to start looking, or the reception she might receive even if she found Alicia.

After all, it had been Beatrice who had changed her name from Festa to Taylor. It was she who had broken off all hope of making contact. And she was still bitterly ashamed of the reason she had done so.

Beatrice stood watching the nuns starting to file out of the convent, heading towards the village for Saturday night gelati.

They had a better social life than she!

She stiffened as two particular nuns walked out through the convent gates. Sister Josephine had aged, and walked a little more slowly now, but it was Sister Catherine at her side who caught Beatrice's attention.

She watched as they passed the baby door, where she'd been left, naked and unwrapped, with the umbilical cord still attached.

They were so deep in conversation that they passed it without so much as a glance. Certainly Sister Catherine didn't notice the slight woman who was watching them, almost willing her to linger, to acknowledge the box, to cast a glance around and see if her daughter was here on her birthday.

Nothing.

'What the hell are you even doing here, Beatrice?' she asked herself, and headed straight back to the rental car that had brought her there.

Beatrice would not be heading into the village.

She was done.

And on the flight back to Bellanisiá Beatrice made a private vow that next year, for her thirtieth, she would go somewhere wonderful. She would make friends and drink Birthday Girl Martinis, which she'd heard about but never tried. She would kiss someone and make love, even if the thought terrified her. She would do anything not to be as cold and as unfeeling as the woman who had birthed her.

Beatrice could feel the snap of her own thawing, and it hurt, but she was determined to do it.

She'd hire a gigolo if she had to.

It was when she arrived back at her little flat on the marina that she broke down.

Oh, she hadn't gone to Trebordi hoping for words of wisdom from her mother—that was a joke—but she ached for a friend, a true friend, to give her some gentle advice.

And yet she had fled.

She stared at the one photo she had from her childhood, desperate for Alicia, who'd always known that behind the façade she was terrified.

In truth, she needed someone to tell her it was just a crush. That the way she felt now, at twenty-nine, was just her catching up on the teenage years she'd missed out on.

More than that, though, she wanted common sense.

But, given she'd stalled at the first hurdle in her search for Alicia, Beatrice had to settle for her own advice.

So what if she liked the Prince a little more than she should?

It would never go anywhere.

He was unattainable.

Impossible.

Safe.

CHAPTER TWO

'*Signorina…*' THE DRIVER greeted Beatrice as she boarded
the shuttle bus with her cup of coffee.

As she made her way down the aisle, a woman Beatrice
recognised from Catering commented in Italian that she
was rarely late.

'*Meglio tardi che mai*—better late than never,' Beatrice
responded, hoping she hadn't noticed her red eyes as she
took her regular seat, second from the back and to the left.

It had become a habit.

'Beatrice?'

She glanced up, and the woman who had commented
on her being late tapped her security lanyard. Beatrice
nodded her thanks, because in her haste she'd forgotten
to put her own on.

Then the guards boarded the bus for an ID check, and
that delayed things more.

By the time she disembarked, though still easily on
time, she felt as if she were running late, and she walked
briskly through the rose garden and past the lake, then
took the steps down to the basement offices.

'There are reports surfacing about a party aboard Prince
Julius's yacht.'

Once—just once—Beatrice would have liked to make
it to her office before being hauled into whatever scandal

the Prince had created. This particular morning, though, she would have also liked to top up her concealer and hide her swollen eyes before facing the world.

She should never have made the short journey to Trebordi, Beatrice knew. Now she felt unsettled, as well as perturbed, and thanks to the evidence her tears had left on her features she felt exposed.

'Thanks, Jordan,' she called to the Prince's overly involved, constantly overwrought PA. 'I'll take a look.'

'Beatrice, wait.' Jordan came out of her downstairs office to further enlighten her. 'Prince Julius is—'

'Oh, please!' Beatrice called over her shoulder, forcing herself to become the aloof, say-it-as-it-is woman she'd been hired to be. 'He's gorgeous, single, and happens to have a sex-life...'

Her voice trailed off as she stepped into her own office and it dawned on her that Jordan had been trying to warn her that she had company.

Royal company.

'Good morning, Beatrice.'

Damn.

There, leaning against the wall, wearing jodhpurs and boots and a very serious expression, was Prince Julius himself. Utterly calm, with his shoulders resting on the wall. But his pose was one of observation rather than relaxation: his arms were folded and his long booted legs lightly crossed.

His glossy ebony hair was messy, his jaw unshaven, although she knew that soon the slight disorder would be righted and he would be polished, groomed and shaved. But for now she dealt with well over six feet of testosterone in jodhpurs, boots and a shirt that suggested he'd exerted both himself and his horse to the full this morning.

Oh, it hadn't been nerves she'd dealt with on first meeting him—not even butterflies, for there was nothing floaty or fluttery about this. Those bats were flapping their wings in her chest again, and she willed them back to their cave. To please hang there quietly and let her get on with her work.

'Your Highness.' Beatrice gave a tight smile.

He didn't return it.

She refused to blush over her comments, or even apologise. After all, it was nothing that Beatrice hadn't already said, either to him or during endless strategy meetings with both his and the King's aides.

'Sir...' Jordan came rushing in as Beatrice put down her work bag and placed her coffee on the desk. 'I can only apologise if we were speaking out of turn...'

'It's fine,' Julius responded. 'Carry on with what you were doing, Jordan.'

As Jordan backed out, Beatrice removed her jacket and placed it over the back of her chair, then faced him. 'To what do I owe the pleasure, sir?'

'I thought we'd addressed the matter of titles,' Julius reminded her. 'We're in your office now.'

God, why had she insisted on dropping titles? He'd agreed that when they were in her office or out walking, as they sometimes were when discussing the more sensitive subjects, she could call him by his name.

Oh, how she ached for strict protocol now. To call him *sir*, to be in his upstairs office, to be groomed and prepared rather than have him land here just after 8:30 a.m.

She felt unprepared—and not just because of her puffy eyes. There was something else. For the first time in her life it *mattered* to Beatrice that she stood there in trainers instead of smart black ballet flats and had her hair scraped back—not that she would be correcting any of those issues with Julius there.

Beatrice closed the door and opened up the blinds, then took a seat.

He did not.

Julius remained leaning against the wall, but not slouching; she doubted a man as elegant as he even knew how to slouch. He just leaned his broad shoulders upon it and watched her. Clearly he was less than impressed by her words on arrival. She could feel the tension in the air.

Fire me, then, Beatrice thought. It would probably be easier.

She chose to reach for her coffee, but after taking a sip pulled a face. 'I knew it.'

He sighed his impatience. 'I don't have time to wait for you to get another.'

'No. It's not that. It's this new cup. It's supposed to keep it warm for up to two hours…' Her voice trailed off as he frowned. What would he know about insulated cups and the shuttle bus for palace staff?

Or it was possible he was frowning because he'd just noticed her swollen eyes.

She reached for a tissue to save herself. 'Excuse me,' she said. 'Allergies.'

'Allergies to what?'

'Personal questions!'

She flashed him a tight smile and then reached into her bag and took out her notebook and pen, as well as her work phone, which she turned on.

'Ooh,' she said, as numerous alerts pinged in. 'You have been busy over the weekend.'

Still he leant against the wall. 'You don't check it at all, do you?'

'What do you mean? I have it on all the time,' Beatrice said, scrolling through the messages, and then added, 'during work hours.'

Her strict adherence to her own rules were, in this client's case, more for her sanity's sake. Constant updates on Julius and his bedroom shenanigans she so did not need! Although, Beatrice conceded, there hadn't been anything too scandalous of late—indeed, he'd kept to his side of the deal and lain low.

His past was another matter, though... Without any new scandals to splash across their front pages, the press were digging up old ones—and there were plenty!

Nessue Respetto!

No respect. That was the subject matter of one of the many articles starting to download.

'"*Re Dezante!*"' Beatrice blinked. 'Dancing King?'

'I'm delighted my brother died, apparently. I am dancing on his grave at the chance to be King.'

She took up the file on her desk, bracing herself for whatever delights awaited. It had never bothered her till now. She'd looked at intimate shots of other clients rather as if she was searching for her horoscope at the back of a magazine, but she knew her lips pursed when the pictures were of him.

There had never been anything sleazy—Julius, even at his most depraved, had always ensured the drapes and luxury suite doors remained closed while he had his wicked way. It was just the odd image that particularly irked— that had Beatrice lying awake at night, frowning into the dark, pondering new mysteries.

Who would kiss someone's feet on a beach? All that sand. Yuck. Why would anyone want to kiss a foot?

Beatrice gave herself a mental shake and reminded herself to keep her face relaxed. She considered adding antacid to her coffee cup, to save her from the burn that hit her sometimes.

'Should I prepare to be shocked?'

'You seem completely unshockable, Beatrice.'

She tried to be, but not this morning...

Re dezante, indeed. Or *principe dezante*—because he wasn't yet King, but this prince could certainly dance.

Gosh, she had never so much as considered that he might.

In the photo he wore black trousers and a black shirt and black boots, and the woman he held was being dipped so low that she was almost lying on the deck of his yacht. Her hair was splayed out on the deck in a puddle of brunette curls and waves.

Beatrice had been anticipating something dreadful, appalling, yet the sight of him fully dressed and just *living*, while she'd spent her birthday weeping, seemed to ram home the fact that it really was time for change.

She blew her nose, to give herself time to school her reaction. She was so jealous of her, the beauty in his arms, and not even for the fact that it was Julius holding her...

It was her abandon. Her trust in the hands that held her.

'You didn't drop her, did you?' Beatrice's voice was croaky as she attempted a joke. 'Are there going to be air ambulances and medics...?'

'What?'

He sounded bemused by her question, and Beatrice reminded herself that quips were not her forte, so she got back to the remaining photos.

No, he hadn't dropped her. There were others dancing too, but the camera had been trained on him, and Beatrice's attention moved to the next shot. The woman was back on her feet, their bodies were locked together, her thigh lifted onto his, and she saw how his hand held her hip. She flicked to another picture, and another, and another...

She wanted to shift in her seat, because she felt discomfort in a place there should not be any. She wanted to rearrange her bra because it felt a size too small all of a sudden.

How could a picture of a fully dressed man do this to her?

Beatrice didn't know.

Yet it did.

He did.

At night, she slept with her hands above her embroidered quilt, as the nuns had insisted. She lay like a lady, desperately wanting to be a woman, fighting the feelings he evoked night after night.

Now, though, those feelings had not only crept into her evenings and mornings. They were following her into work—rather like the white peacock who startled her some mornings and provided an unwelcome escort, trailing his feathers behind him...

Make it stop, Beatrice thought.

The Prince's scent was not that of the stables, but citrussy and fresh, and she felt as if there must be a neon sign over her head with an arrow pointing to the effect he was having on her. She dared not look up, so she stared at the images instead.

'Did they get any photos after...?'

She felt a little shaken, which was exactly what she had been hired *not* to be.

'After...?' he checked.

After the extended foreplay, she wanted to say, but thankfully remained silent.

'God, no. It was nothing like that. We were just dancing,' Julius said, and Beatrice wished she could question his choice of the word *just*, because the images were so sensual and graceful and compelling. 'Admittedly,' he added, 'I don't know how we got onto Latin American, but clearly we did…'

'Clearly.'

Now she had another thing to add to her thirtieth birthday. Even if she didn't go through with it, Beatrice wanted to add dancing to that phantom list for that phantom night.

She tried to haul her mind from Cuban-heeled boots and all the other things she'd never done, yet which somehow Julius had made her consider.

And she didn't quite know why.

Arrogant, haughty, cutting—that didn't even *begin* to describe him.

He was so *unrepentant*.

So contrary.

For he could be so rigid and formal, yet conversely so at ease with himself.

And so damned sexy too—which was the very reason she was employed, after all.

And, although he was supposed to be lying low, they could hardly ban dancing—although Beatrice did have one genuine concern.

'These are seriously good photos.'

'Thank you.'

'I mean they weren't taken on a phone. These are professional shots. How did anyone get close enough to take them? Where was your security?'

'There were boats all around. My mistake.'

'Well, I don't see any issue. It just looks like you enjoyed your weekend.'

'The issue is…' There was a pause, a rare beat of reticence, before he spoke on. 'They weren't taken at the weekend.'

For the first time since meeting him she sensed his discomfort. 'So?'

'These were taken on the first anniversary...' He paused. 'Of Claude's death.'

She thought back to the wooden, formal man she had met at her final interview, then looked at the photos, and struggled to reconcile the two men. Perhaps she was starting to know him better...

Know him?

A tiny bit. Enough to understand that these headlines hurt him, even if he would never admit it.

'Okay.' Beatrice looked again at the pictures, with this new information on board. 'So, these were taken on the anniversary of Prince Claude's death.'

'Yes, I attended a formal service that morning—though apparently I was faking my solemn mood then.'

'So, you're only allowed one emotion a day?'

Beatrice raised her eyebrows and he gave a silent, mirthless half-laugh, as if relieved that she got it.

Lately, she did.

Beatrice herself had only used to feel two things: cold and lonely.

Now she felt as if she were juggling a hundred or more emotions and feelings, while trying to find her old favourite: cold. That way she would be able to see objectively what they were dealing with.

She turned to her computer and tried to access the files of photos taken on the anniversary of Claude's death.

Limited Access.

'What's wrong?' he asked as she gritted her teeth.

'I have to go upstairs to access the archives.'

Her security clearance at the palace allowed for little more than a schoolgirl doing a project; it was easier to go online along with the general population. She found a couple of shots of that day: the Queen looked her usual poised and elegant self, though the black jewels in her diadem sparkled far more vividly than her tired eyes; Princess Jasmine, Julius's older sister in a rare public appearance, was hidden behind a black veil and holding her daughter Arabella's hand, and the King…he was austere and sombre. But then, from what she had gleaned he'd always been austere and sombre, as well as scathing, where his youngest was concerned.

As for Julius… He stood on ceremony, but behind those dark eyes, who knew what went on?

Sometimes, lately, Beatrice felt as if she did, just a little.

Most of the time, lately, she wanted to.

Wanted to know.

Yet now, seeing a photo of him taken just a few weeks ago caused her to frown, and she looked over to where he stood. He'd lost weight in the weeks she'd been here. Not a lot. It was almost indiscernible. But he certainly had.

There was also a new tension to his features that hadn't been present even on that sombre anniversary.

She looked back to the photo and found herself nibbling on her bottom lip as she thought.

Was the soon-to-be groom having pre-selection jitters? Certainly he hadn't signed the Document of Intent that would kick things off, and even she could feel the pressure building from the palace for him to do so. Or was he just antsy from being forced to leave his normal life behind?

Julius broke into her thoughts. 'It was careless,' he admitted. 'I was just…'

'Just?'

'I suppose the term would be *letting off steam.*'

'I get it,' Beatrice said.

Last night, as she'd wept, it had felt as if a valve had been released—just a touch. She'd quickly turned it back to closed. Only it felt as if she hadn't quite managed to secure that valve, because the steam seemed to be hissing out despite her attempts to shut it off completely.

'I don't dance, of course, but—'

'You don't dance?'

'No.'

'At all?' He sounded surprised.

'No, but what I meant...' What *did* she mean? She didn't dance. 'I'm saying that I understand that we all have our outlets.'

Beatrice's outlets were studying languages and embroidery...

Julius peeled his broad shoulders from the wall and came and took a seat on the other side of her desk. He looked at her as he stretched out his legs.

'Why don't you dance, Beatrice?' He remained curious.

Can we get back to the photos, please? she wanted to beg, but Julius seemed intrigued by her little slip.

'I was never taught,' she snapped. 'Were you?'

'Absolutely.' He nodded. 'We had lessons in the ballroom...'

'The three of you?' Beatrice couldn't stop herself asking.

He nodded. 'We had costumes and everything.'

'Did you hate it?'

'Not at all.'

She'd expected him to grimace, to pull a face, but he surprised her. Many times in their short history Julius had surprised her, and he did so now.

'I loved it.' He leant back in his chair and clasped his hands behind his head, resting there as he thought for a moment. 'Claude and Jasmine loathed it...' He smiled to himself at the memory. 'My father was worried I liked it a little too much!'

Beatrice resisted the smile that ached to spread across her face and reminded herself that she was cold and impassive as Julius spoke on.

'As well as ballroom, there was *syrtaki*, tarantella… Oh, and there was *horon*.'

'*Horon?*'

'It's a folk dance, from the Black Sea. My mother's side…' He raised his arms and dropped his wrists. 'Like Irish dancing with your hands in the air. Great fun.'

Her lips started to spread, and then of their own accord they parted, and she didn't know how to take it off, this smile that remained on her face.

This was the part of Julius she didn't understand, because at times it felt as if he *chose* to make her smile. Sometimes it honestly felt as if he'd made a decision to remain in a conversation with her in order to challenge himself to put a smile upon her face. Then, when he succeeded, when there was no doubt the smile on her face was a genuine one, he returned it.

It was as simple and as un-noteworthy as that. Yet there was something else she couldn't properly explain…something indefinable.

It was not just that he *chose* to make her smile but that on a day like today, when she felt so out of step with the rest of the world, when she felt she must surely be the most unlovable person ever, somehow he *found* her smile.

And returned it.

When it had faded, he asked, 'Is everything okay, Beatrice?'

'Of course.' She nodded, removing her eyes from his and trying to remember where they'd left the conversation. 'What about Latin American?'

'Sorry?'

She gestured with her palm towards the spread of disturbingly erotic photos gracing her desk this morning.

'Ah, I believe I had one-on-one tuition for that. That really is filed under "Limited Access".'

'You're dreadful,'

'I try to be.'

She felt his eyes upon her and looked up from the images of him dancing to the darkest eyes, which had narrowed just a little. Beatrice reminded herself that she was at work—that he could have been dancing naked on the palace balcony and her job would be to fix the situation.

Back to the issue.

'Okay… Prince Claude's anniversary coincided with the start of the Hellenic celebrations?' She cross-checked the dates.

'It did.'

'So that's why there were so many boats all around?'

'Yes.'

'Have you discussed this with Security?'

'I'll deal with that side of things. All I want from you is to know how best to respond.'

'Of course. Is it a tradition that you go each year?'

'No,' Julius dismissed, then added, 'Claude did, though. It was his favourite thing.'

'That's good. Could it be that you wanted to honour his *joie de vivre* by going in his place?'

'Don't go there,' Julius warned. 'I won't use him as an excuse. And anyway…' he mused with a mixture of pensiveness and affection. 'There was not a lot of *joie de vivre* to Claude. He really was rather staid.'

She glanced up at the shift in his tone. He'd confided in her!

Beatrice wanted to stand on her chair and point! To call her missing friend to help her name this feeling.

Beatrice would have liked to understand this moment, because these rare insights felt like something so precious, so rare—like nothing she could find out from her colleagues or hours on the computer...

'Actually...' Julius too seemed to realise this veer from the norm, for he added, 'Don't go repeating that!'

'That' felt as if it was just for them. But she blinked herself out of any delusions by looking again at his beautiful dance partner and reminding herself that he would be married soon. And anyway, she had no idea about men.

None.

Just the dreadful ones whose chaotic private lives needed her ice-cold touch.

And so she gave it now.

'I suggest "no comment" to the photos.'

In her time here at the palace she had held fast to her strategy, and there had been no comments nor apologies made following any tabloid pictures of the Prince.

'Actually,' Julius said. 'In this instance I'm not sure.'

This was a rare moment of indecision on his part. So rare that Beatrice had actually never seen the doubt that now flashed over his features.

'Does it merit an apology?' he asked.

'No.'

'A response?'

'No.'

'Because if it does...'

'Julius, no.' Beatrice was adamant, almost cross in his defence. 'You've lost your *brother.* If dancing helps, then please...' she raised her hands '...sign me up for the classes...'

'Thanks.' He gave a half-laugh at her honest and unusually passionate response. 'I always forget you're Sicilian.'

'Oh, believe me, I try to.'

Beatrice wanted to take that back. It wasn't Sicily she wanted to forget—it was one woman. She knew he'd seen that little flash of venom, but thankfully he politely ignored it as she dived into her work bag.

'I should have some…'

'What?'

'Antihistamines…' Beatrice knew there were none there, and nor did she need them; she just wanted to hide for a tiny second. 'I must have left them at home.'

'That's not like you.'

No. 'Well, leave everything with me.' She gave him a tight smile and really hoped he'd take the cue and leave. She had never felt less together at work than she did this morning.

But he did not get up and he did not leave. 'They're going to keep serving this stuff up,' he said.

'The press?'

'Whoever… The longer I leave it, the more this stuff will appear to undermine me.'

'Undermine?' Beatrice frowned. 'No…'

Oh, no! Undermine? Under *him*, more likely! That would probably be the thought flickering across minds this morning. But, no, this photo wouldn't damage Julius, if that was their game.

'I don't think you have to worry about that.'

'Well, you can expect a lot of this kind of stuff to keep appearing until I sign the Document of Intent.' He inhaled and closed his eyes. 'Or the Point of No Return…' He looked over and gave a half-smile. 'Joking.'

But he had not been joking. His mask, too, had briefly slipped. It was the first time he had spoken of his destined future with anything other than crisp certainty.

'What happens then?' Beatrice asked, as if she were mildly curious instead of completely relieved that she hadn't found out and wouldn't, given that her contract was soon to expire. 'It was all supposed to be happening before I left, but...'

'I sign the Document of Intent, it goes to counsel, and after about a month or so I find out who they've chosen.'

'Do you have any idea who?'

'None.'

'None?'

'It could be someone from a country we're aligned with, or one with whom we need to broker better relations. My parents' union was heralded as one of the country's greatest, even if no one here had heard of her country prior to the marriage. My mother is the most esteemed queen consort in centuries... So who knows?' Julius shrugged. 'And then, once the decision is made, the marriage will take place within a month, assuming all parties are agreed.'

'Do you get to meet each other beforehand?'

'Of course. The families will dine together a week before...' He put up a hand to show it wasn't a certain thing. 'Depending on her country and their traditions, of course.'

'You'll speak the same language?'

'Not necessarily. My parents didn't. Hey, there might be a position for a translator when your contract...' He halted, just for a fraction of a second, but then shrugged. 'Well, given your skill set...'

Sometimes she thought she was imagining things, but that little pause had felt as if it contained a wealth of information. That he might find the idea of Beatrice joining him on his honeymoon as an appalling thought as she did.

It was by far more sensible not to dwell on it.

'My mother spoke only Romeyka when they were first married, and my father's never quite mastered it. Nor me.

And I'm supposed to be addressing her family at the end of the week, when I visit.'

'Well, if you need to practise I'm good with languages. Not that one, but I know some of the sounds.'

'I'll be fine.' He rejected her offer to assist and got back to the question. 'After the wedding, there'll be a month on Regalsi, so we can get to know each other...' He must have seen her frown. 'It's one of the tiny islands—just for royals.'

'What's it like?'

'I've never been. It's for honeymoons and hetaerae and such...'

'Mistresses?'

'We don't use that word here,' he warned with a shush and a smile. 'Regalsi's a place for serious relationships— and *that's* why I've never been.'

It bemused her a little. Julius, from all she could see, had had longer term relationships, but though he spoke of his exes politely, even fondly, there had never been one considered serious enough to join him at formal functions, nor, it would seem, to take to Regalsi.

Julius interrupted her thoughts. 'I have to say, with the way my schedule is, an entire month off is starting to sound tempting.'

'That's not very romantic.'

'It isn't about romance. It's about a partnership.'

He turned his head at the sound of a voice outside her door.

'Knock-knock?'

'It would seem you have a visitor,' he said to Beatrice, and called for Jordan to come in.

And this morning, when she wanted only to hide, Jordan came in carrying a cake lit with candles and the rest of the team all shuffled in behind her.

'Cake?' Beatrice was startled.

'Palace cake,' Jordan corrected.

So that was why he'd hung around making small talk. And that was why he hadn't wanted her to go and get more coffee. He was being polite.

She smiled as Jordan placed on her desk the prettiest cake she'd ever seen. It had a meadow of flowers delicately piped on it, as well as...

'My name!'

'Of course.'

There was no 'of course' about it.

A birthday cake with candles and her name on it was a first for Beatrice, and very overwhelming.

Growing up in the convent, there had been a simple square honey cake for supper on the children's birthdays, and that had felt like such a treat.

She watched as Tobias, Julius's private aide, placed two cards on her desk and listened as Jordan explained.

'It was made especially by the head pastry chef. Technically, we only do it for permanent staff, but...'

'Well, that will never happen.' Beatrice offered her usual smart response just as she saw Jordan notice her red eyes.

'Gosh, you really celebrated at the weekend, didn't you?'

Was she so removed from everyone that Jordan assumed she must have a crashing hangover from partying because it had never occurred to her that she might have been crying?

'Come on, Beatrice,' Julius snapped. 'Are you going to cut it?'

'Of course.'

She took up the knife and aimed it at the cake.

'Candles first,' Julius warned.

'Oh, yes...' She puffed them out.

God, she was useless—so useless that after a couple of dreadful attempts at slicing Tobias rescued the knife from her unskilled hand and took over.

'How was your weekend?' asked Despina, who was head of social media for the Prince. 'You went home, didn't you?'

'It was fine,' Beatrice answered.

'Did you catch up with your family?'

'I guess…'

'So,' Tobias asked, 'how was Sicily?'

'Windy,' she responded, and searched for anything she could think of to deflect the questioning. 'How's Esther? You've got the ultrasound today, yes?'

Beatrice knew what she was doing. Tobias's wife was pregnant, and there was nothing better to halt an unwanted question than to invite someone else to speak—especially someone looking forward to being a father.

'Yes! We should find out what we're having…'

Tobias chatted happily on, and out of the corner of her eye she watched as Julius went to reach for the last piece of cake, then reluctantly checked himself.

'Does anyone want this?' he offered, clearly still hungry from riding and ready to take the last of the cake and get on with his busy day.

'I do,' Beatrice said.

He halted.

So did Beatrice. Because suddenly there was something wrong with her voice. Something that made him look over.

No one else seemed aware of it, but it caused him to screw up his very straight nose just a fraction at being thwarted and rather petulantly take back his hand.

'Of course.' He nodded and shot her a look that somehow caused her stomach, as well as an area lower, to clench. 'After all, it's your cake.'

'It is,' Beatrice said, and somehow held his gaze.

'Enjoy!' Jordan half laughed and half scolded as he went sulking out of her office, but Beatrice just stood there, wondering what had happened. For a second there it had felt as if there was no one else in her tiny office.

Just one last slice of cake and him.

Oh, God, had he thought she was flirting?

Had she been?

Had he?

Had they?

Beatrice didn't know.

She had never tuned in to such things—let alone had to tune out. Before arriving here she'd thought that flirting was all batting eyelashes and bumping into each other at every turn, but it would appear that the opposite might be the case. They usually seemed to sit or stand as far from each other as possible. Something had happened there, though…

As the rest of the staff wandered out Jordan closed the door behind them and her smile disappeared. 'Beatrice, you have to be more careful.'

'With…?'

Had she noticed? Was she going to be told off for flirting with the Prince?

No, it was her words on arrival that she was being chastised for, as Beatrice quickly found out.

'How was I supposed to know he was here?' she asked.

'I was trying to warn you. This is *his* residence…' Jordan closed her eyes in exasperation for a brief moment. 'I know he doesn't usually come down here, but you have to be more guarded with your words.'

'You're not,' Beatrice retorted.

As his PA, Jordan was Beatrice's main source of information and, Beatrice thought, rather indiscreet.

'The door is closed, Beatrice,' Jordan pointed out, and then asked for the Prince's take on the photos. 'What's he going to do about them?'

'Nothing,' Beatrice said, and opened up a window. 'God, the place is going to reek of the stables...'

'I don't smell it,' Jordan said. 'Mind you, Stavros used to work there...'

Beatrice knew only too well that Stavros, Jordan's husband, had worked at the stables. Jordan talked about her marriage so fondly and freely that Beatrice felt as if she had already met him!

Still, it wasn't the smell of the stables that she wanted *out*; it was the scent of Julius that she wanted to gulp *in*. It felt as if there were a fire behind her, truly. But there were no alarms, no ladders against the wall, no passers-by to wave to for help. Nothing to show or recount.

Even Jordan was oblivious. 'I think, in this case, he ought to at least consider an apology.'

The fact that Julius had wondered the same thing would remain with Beatrice. 'Well, I don't think it's necessary—and I'll tell the King's aides the same.'

'This won't go away,' Jordan warned. 'Look, I'm only saying this to you,' she said, which Beatrice didn't believe for a second, 'but I've heard a whisper that they're discussing sending him to rehab.'

'Why on earth would they even suggest such a thing? He's the healthiest person I've ever met.'

'It's a battle of wills,' Jordan said. 'Julius won't go, of course, but he might agree to sign the Document of Intent if they threaten him with it. Honestly, you'd think he'd have more sense than to go out partying on the anniversary of his brother's death. It's not a good look.'

'He was probably just trying to get through the day.'

'And the night.' Jordan rolled her eyes. 'In his usual fashion, no doubt.'

'Well, at least he's lying low now. This is all old stuff.'

'Old?' Jordan checked. 'Claude's anniversary was in June—just a couple of months ago.'

'I meant it was before my time.'

The thought afforded her too much relief. One day— today, tomorrow, who knew when?—she would be sitting here looking at images of Julius and his current lover and discussing more recent scandals.

Better that, though, than looking at an image of his chosen bride.

'I should go,' Jordan said. 'Enjoy!' She gestured to Beatrice's slice of cake and her cards. 'I'd better get on.'

'Jordan?' Beatrice halted her. 'I don't like this gossip about rehab.'

'Of course not. That's why I told you about it.'

Oh.

With Jordan headed to the more sumptuous floors above, and everyone gone from her office, Beatrice stared at the near empty cake plate and the candles that had been lit for her. She was still a bit stunned, because she just didn't do birthdays. Avoided them.

She opened her cards—the pink one first. It was signed by all the Prince's team.

Hope you had a brilliant time celebrating!

That was the general theme. And they hoped that her trip to Sicily had been amazing. That was the other.

The Big Thirty next year, Jordan had reminded her, and added a smiley face.

And then Beatrice took up a letter opener and carefully sliced open the big creamy envelope with her name written on it in Jordan's handwriting, and pulled out the most exquisite card.

It was a beautiful black and white shot of the Prince's residence with the White Lake in the foreground. It deserved to be in a frame on the wall in its own right.

She opened the card and saw the flash of his scrawl above his printed name and title, and then she glanced at the piece of cake.

Why did it have to be like this?

It was a simple crush.

On HRH.

It was purely physical, but her body—which knew nothing about men—seemed to be coming to life around him. She was flustered at work…perhaps for the first time.

Thank goodness she could now gather herself in private.

But suddenly he was back!

'Beatrice? Actually, those pictures seem to be turning into an issue. I'm going to have to meet with my father's aides later.'

'I can do that,' Beatrice said. After all, she did it most days. 'You've got enough to be doing.'

'No, I'll meet you up there when they call for me.'

She nodded.

He was turning to go and then he glanced to the last remaining piece of cake and then to her. For the first time ever both his gaze and a slow smile combined and homed in on her.

It was like being invited to witness a private viewing of the sun.

No wonder her services were required.

No wonder he had caused so much trouble.

'Just take it,' Beatrice snapped.

Julius didn't wait to be asked twice. He walked over and picked up the piece of cake and took a bite.

Her insides felt as if they were melting faster than the cream he licked from those decadent lips before walking out with his prize.

Oh, why did it have to be like this?

CHAPTER THREE

'THE PALACE ARE *insisting* on a response,' Jordan told him.

'Well, they can keep on insisting.' Julius shrugged.

They were upstairs in the office with the door closed. Second only to Tobias, he trusted Jordan, for though it was never spoken out loud she knew the real pressure he was under.

'I'm just relaying what I've heard, sir.'

He nodded. 'Beatrice is on it.'

'Hungover to the back teeth,' Jordan retorted. 'I'm sorry about this morning, sir.'

'Drop it,' Julius said, rather than point out to her that she'd been crying.

He'd easily seen that his usually very together liaison aide was unusually reactive today. Her lips were chewed, her nose red, and she'd been nattering on about cups and such when usually she barely said an unnecessary word.

A family drama, perhaps?

Or a relationship break-up, maybe?

He didn't get involved with the personal dramas of his staff. If he did he'd never get a single thing done. Well, he tried not to get involved. God knows, he tried.

The same way he'd tried not to notice her red eyes.

And tried not to be irked that he was something confined

to her work bag and taken out on her arrival at the palace on a Monday, like a schoolteacher with his homework.

He'd tried to make inane small talk with her as agreed, while Jordan gathered the rest of the team and brought in the cake, but he had started to slip away from small talk.

That would never do.

He did his best to be present for team birthdays, but would usually grab one slice of cake and then go. Yet he'd seen she was struggling, standing there as if not knowing quite what to do instead of blowing out the candles and slicing. So he'd moved things along. She'd sounded surprised by the direction in conversation.

It had quickly become evident that cutting cake wasn't one of Beatrice's talents; in fact her knife skills were so bad that Tobias had relieved her of cutting duties. But at least Julius had managed to scoop up one of Beatrice's attempts—a big slice—and then watched as she'd deflected questions.

Beatrice, Julius had found out, revealed nothing about herself.

Ever.

He made small talk with strangers, was skilled in negotiations, but he'd got nowhere with Beatrice. She was impenetrable.

Beatrice had not brightened either the walls of her office or her desk with personal touches. Whether she worked upstairs in his main offices or down here, everything personal was returned to that vast bag at the end of the day and no traces were left.

She didn't wear perfume; in fact, her choice of soap and shampoo was even a little carbolic in nature. Like… antiseptic.

Warding off germy men? he mused.

But then this morning he'd found out that she didn't dance.

And that sometimes she cried.

He read women, adored women—that was the reason she was here, after all—and a lot of his time was spent deflecting advances—hopefully nicely.

Beatrice had made no advances.

And nor would he.

She was staff, so of course it was impossible. Though that would be remedied in three long weeks—and he would be away for one of those, thank God.

Also, he did not want to add to the poor opinion she clearly had of him, or be like those creeps she had worked for in the past.

Plus, soon his bride would be chosen.

Ah, that!

What had always been a necessary duty now felt like a weight—a weight he would like to discard, at least for a night.

Preferably with the woman hired to clean up his image.

He'd seen how she held herself back from all the team; she even ate lunch at the lake instead of in the staffroom with everyone else.

She'd revealed nothing.

Not a sign, nor a clue.

And then, out of the blue, she'd denied him cake…

'I do.'

It hadn't been the words—nor even the delivery.

And no one else had seemed to hear it quite as he had.

Oh, they had no doubt heard her teasing tone alongside her usual assertiveness, because they had laughed. And yet no one had seemed to catch what was bubbling beneath the surface.

The shell of his ear had felt as if she had just leaned in and whispered a promise.

Those two words had hit him where it should hurt, and

yet they had felt at light and as potent as the stroke of an intimate finger—so much so that he had felt himself tighten in response.

He was rarely mistaken. She'd made no further advance, given no other clue, and yet he *almost* knew.

And he would find out.

In three weeks' time Beatrice Taylor would leave the palace.

Perhaps one discreet liaison with his liaison aide before he joined the monogamy club…?

'Sir?' Jordan's nervous swallow alerted him and he looked up. 'Is this latest revelation perhaps…'

'Because I haven't signed the Document of Intent?' He said it for her. 'I would think so.'

The publication of those photos was no accident; the pressure was all from within.

'Sir, do you remember I suggested offering Beatrice a full-time role here?'

'Beatrice isn't going to stop them.' He shook his head. 'No.'

Hell, no.

She was the damned reason he hadn't signed it. He would like to get to back to business—certainly not offer her a permanent role. On the permanent staff? Always there? Always by his side?

Yikes. God, no.

'Julius.' Jordan actually snapped his name. 'If Beatrice was permanent then she'd have clearance, and at least she'd know what you're up against.'

'And what would that change?'

'Please…just listen.'

And because it was Jordan's responsibility to deal with such matters, he had no choice but to listen as she pointed out how much more smoothly things had been going since

Beatrice's arrival. That it had been Beatrice who had sat through many, many meetings arguing his case, without him there.

She added, 'Even though I'm a little loath to admit it.'

'Loath?' Julius checked. 'You were the one who pushed for her selection.'

'I did.' Jordan nodded. 'And she's great at her job.'

'But…?'

'I do have my reservations… Take this morning.'

'Yep.'

He got up from his seat and looked down at the lake, listening to Jordan's brusque summing up of his icy, albeit efficient liaison aide.

'And she's not exactly a team player,' Jordan said. 'But that's not your issue.'

It was, though.

Julius felt as if Beatrice *was* on his team.

Beatrice Taylor was exceedingly good at her job.

Why the hell *wouldn't* he keep her on?

He knew why.

She was the coldest, most direct, private and prickly woman he'd ever met—but she could also be suddenly kind.

It hadn't been long after her arrival at the palace that he had found that she fascinated him. He'd found himself leaning against the window, pondering a problem, and had noticed her tipping some crumbs into the lake and one of the gardeners dashing over to scold her.

Julius hadn't really noticed then; it had been but an idle observation. It was the next day that he'd looked down and watched her open a container and wave at the gardener, who'd returned her wave.

He'd found himself smiling.

Not just that day but a little more often since then.

He'd noticed that her eyes were more grey than blue, and framed with blonde lashes.

Julius had chosen to ignore the fact that he'd noticed.

But Julius wanted her to stay—after all, he could really use her skill set.

Practically, he knew he wouldn't be able to tolerate anyone else glimpsing his private life without it feeling invasive, and he knew by objecting he would be denying her the chance of an excellent promotion.

But privately?

There was no room for private.

No room at all.

And, as if to serve as a reminder of exactly what was at stake, when he looked down now it wasn't Beatrice by the lake. It was his sister Jasmine, feeding the birds with Arabella. He adored his niece, but she was so loud and so spoilt he thought she'd possibly put him off having kids for life!

He loved them, though.

And his father knew it.

It was a Sword of Damocles that his father held over Julius's head and with which he ruled his family.

Perhaps it was time to stop thinking primitive thoughts and get on with fulfilling the role he'd been born to—well, not born to, but born *just in case* to…

'Let me think on it,' he said now.

He had enough to deal with today, Julius realised.

The King was currently meeting his aides. Then the aides would discuss the situation, and then they would call him in.

'Sir, I've moved things around. The meeting is at three,' Jordan informed him, and then added, 'It's just with the aides.'

Julius nodded. All too soon it would be with the King.

Julius's dark mood now had nothing to do with his li-aison aide.

He called Beatrice and said, 'I want you to come up with a bland response to these latest photos. I'll meet you in the Great Hall at three.' Then he added, 'Don't be early.'

He would not be bullied.

CHAPTER FOUR

HE'D DANCED! Yes, on the anniversary of his brother's death…

It was a minor infringement in the scheme of Julius's rather more decadent deeds. In driving terms, Beatrice would have likened it to the equivalent of a blown headlight, yet it was as if his staff were preparing for an appearance in court for vehicular manslaughter.

'Can I read the response?' Tobias came in half an hour before they were scheduled to meet.

'Sure,' Beatrice said, and handed him the paper.

'This is the press release?'

Beatrice nodded.

'No.' He shook his head. 'It says nothing.'

'That's the whole point, Tobias.'

Poor Tobias should be heading home to his pregnant wife, but it was clear he was conflicted and anxious as he re-read it. 'It needs more work.'

'Fine.' She gave him a tight smile as he scurried off.

Beatrice stared at it for another five minutes, added a comma and then deleted it, then got on with other work until Jordan called down.

'The King has just left so they're almost ready.'

'Sure,' Beatrice said. 'Julius said to meet him there at three.'

'Head over now, and call me if anything happens?'

'Anything?' Beatrice checked as she reached for her jacket.

'If they ask for scribes or…' Jordan sighed. 'Just keep me up to date.'

It was a good ten-minute walk from her office in Julius's residence to the palace. Beatrice considered using the catering passage, as she had before on occasion, but Julius had been insistent that she not be early.

So she walked through the glass passageway, but immediately regretted it, for as she came into the main palace there was the King—so like Julius—standing there, looking up at a portrait no doubt of his late son.

Damn.

She knew he would not notice her, so she put her head down as she passed and was duly ignored. She descended the grand staircase and arrived in the Great Hall to find Julius not there and Tobias pacing.

He pulled her into an archway and brought her up to speed. 'They've just called for refreshments,' Tobias said. 'We could be here ages. You might get that royal wedding on your résumé sooner than you think.'

'All because he…danced?'

'You've seen the headlines.'

'Are you saying the wedding could be announced today?'

'If he agrees.' Tobias was seriously rattled. 'You know why you were hired. They want him married and producing heirs.'

Yes, she knew, and although it all felt very different now from when she'd first been given the brief, Beatrice was a professional, and when she worked she was always calm.

'Tobias, they can hardly drag him up the aisle kicking and screaming.'

Suddenly Julius was at her elbow. He must have heard

her because he said, 'I don't kick.' He pointed a finger. 'And I'd certainly never scream. Watch your words.'

Watch your finger, she wanted to retort, but then he decided to do that without her instruction.

He was suited and clean-shaven and just too beautiful for a Monday afternoon.

'Have you got the response?' he asked.

'I have.' She handed him the very brief statement only because she knew the palace had insisted on one. Otherwise they would put out their own. 'I've kept it bland.'

'I like bland,' he said, and read it out loud. '"Prince Julius enjoyed partaking in the commencement of the Hellenic Festival and celebrating our rich Greek heritage." Perfect,' he said. 'We'll go with that.'

Tobias, it would seem, wanted a little more of an apology in there. 'Perhaps wait till the meeting, sir?' he suggested.

'Aren't you supposed to be off now? An ultrasound or something? I think Esther needs her hand holding more than I do,' Julius said. 'Go.'

Beatrice could see that Tobias was torn. This really wasn't about a night of dancing, she was fast realising. It was a push to get the reluctant Prince to instruct the palace to select a bride.

'We're finding out what we're having today,' Julius said once Tobias had left.

'Sorry?'

'That was a little joke, Beatrice.'

She frowned.

'I meant we'll all know tomorrow if it's a boy or girl. The royal *we*…the office *we*…' He gave in, clearly remembering that Beatrice didn't joke. 'Tobias is worried,' Julius admitted. 'Apparently they're discussing a stint in rehab for me in there.'

'Where did he hear that?'

'It doesn't matter.'

'Well, it does, because I'm hearing it too.'

'From…?'

She shook her head.

'I have an ear in the stables…' he said. Then, 'Why does that make you smile?'

'It's fine. I think we might have the same ear.'

Clearly Jordan had confided in both of them. Beatrice must have let her initial worry about Jordan's loose lips show on her face, because he added, 'It's okay. Seriously, you don't have to worry.'

Beatrice said nothing.

'You have to know who to trust, Beatrice,' he told her.

'I do,' Beatrice responded. 'And I've never let myself down yet.'

'I love your constant cynicism, Beatrice.'

'You're relying on it,' she told him. 'While I might be "Limited Access", I know there's more going on.'

'Very well. The palace want to let it be known that I haven't been dealing well with Claude's death.'

'No.' Beatrice shook her head. 'Absolutely not.'

'I agree. It's just a threat so that I'll relent.'

'Relent?'

'I've told them I won't marry on the orders of my father. I don't like being told what to do. It might get a bit heated in there,' he warned. 'And by "it" I mean me.'

She had never seen him nervous, no matter what the scandal—and there had been many. He was usually insolent or arrogant. But he seemed different this Monday afternoon.

She looked at his jet-black hair and the dark brown eyes and the sulky mouth as he examined the portraits that lined the Great Hall; he arched his neck, which she had noticed was his habit when he was tense.

'Julius…'

'Not now,' he said.

'Let me speak first in there.'

'No, thank you.'

He went and sat on one of the polished benches and stretched out his long legs, then he nodded his head at her, indicating for her to join him.

'I'm fine standing, thank you, sir.'

'Please sit,' he said.

It would be far easier to stand—especially as her heart was thumping in her chest—but she perched herself a suitable distance from him. And as she took her place on the bench, she was assailed by a memory.

It was so sharp that she felt almost transported back to happier times—not that they'd felt happy then. She remembered two little girls sitting on a bench, waiting to see what Alicia had done. The memory was so vivid that Beatrice let out a small, almost silent laugh.

'What?' asked Julius.

'It's honestly nothing.'

'Distract me,' he said.

'I was just thinking how I used to sit outside Reverend Mother's room with my…' She faltered, unsure what to say, because she rarely got as far as saying this.

'With your…?'

'Well, we called each other twins, but really we weren't even related.'

'Oh?' He looked over. 'Good friends, then? Or, as my niece would say, *best* friends?'

'Yes…' Beatrice smiled. 'We were.'

'Arabella has just fallen out with hers.'

'Poor thing.'

'I have to say, from all she's told me, it sounds very fraught.'

'She's spoken to you about it?'

'Loudly.' He nodded. 'And then tearfully, when I pointed out she was in the wrong.' He put his head back on the wall behind him. 'Thankfully I've always avoided all that.'

'Didn't you ever have a best friend?'

'God, no,' he said.

'Oh.' She couldn't imagine her childhood without Alicia—or rather, she didn't want to imagine how it might have been without her friend by her side.

He removed his head from the wall and stared ahead. 'If I had I might have spilled palace secrets or something dreadful.'

'Well, I guess there is that to consider.'

'Not really. I doubt my niece and her little friend give a damn about the future of the monarchy.'

He was cross; she could feel it.

And she was nervous about going into the meeting, Beatrice realised.

For him.

There was so much more going on than she was allowed to know. Her 'Limited Access' truly limited her access, and there was no one here who was going to enlighten a temporary employee.

It was Julius who broke the strained silence. 'So,' he asked, 'was it your attitude?'

She frowned, confused by the question.

'I mean, was your attitude the reason you were hauled in front of Reverend Mother.'

'I was the star pupil, actually,' Beatrice corrected. 'It was more a case of guilt by association. Alicia was always in trouble.'

'So, you were the good twin?'

She nodded, but then thought for a moment. 'Actually, even though Alicia might have been the naughty one, she was far nicer than me.'

'Nicer?'

'Yes.'

'Nicer?' he checked again.

'I could be mean. Well, according to Alicia.' She shrugged, intending to end the introspection, but found she lingered there. 'I was jealous, maybe.'

'Of...?'

Many things—from Alicia's gold earrings to the ease of her smile and the way she made friends with strangers. How, even if Beatrice had been the so-called 'clever one', Alicia had always known what to do.

'She had lovely gold earrings.'

'Oh?'

'Turns out I'm allergic to gold.'

'No?'

'Yes, I come up in welts. Still, she was right; I could be mean.' She shrugged. 'You know what girls can be like.'

He didn't, particularly. But he would like to know what this woman was like. There was a potentially life-changing meeting ahead of him, but it was forgotten for now.

For Beatrice truly fascinated him.

She was seriously beautiful. Yet it was not immediately obvious that her beauty ran deep beneath the surface too. He hadn't seen it at first.

In truth, it had irritated him that he'd needed to employ her in the first place. The necessity of employing someone to handle his private life had naturally irked him. It had, at first, felt like an invasion. Yet she was brilliant at her job. Rarely did he have to meet with his father's aides now; he had started to comfortably leave all that to Beatrice.

Julius liked how she'd said upfront that she didn't care what he did and that his private life was his own. He liked her impassive features and the fact that to her he was like a phone to turn on, on a Monday—a schedule to arrange in her notebook.

When had his irritation started to grate on him in another way?

How had it shifted so that he wanted those lips to part and smile, or to hear her laugh?

When had the gap between Friday and Monday started to stretch…?

When had he discovered it was *her* private life that he wanted to dwell upon?

He wished he had paid better attention to her résumé, so that he could better understand how the very English Beatrice was in fact Sicilian. Her well-schooled voice, her education, told him she came from a well-to-do family…

Julius wanted to cheat. When Jordan had discussed offering Beatrice a full-time position, he had wanted to ask for her file. But he hadn't.

Julius found he wanted to hear it from her own pinched lips. He wanted the prim and uptight Beatrice to open up a little to him.

'I'm going to find out what's causing the delay,' she told him, but he shook his head.

'Don't.'

She swallowed and sat back down.

'So, you were the star pupil at a convent school?' he asked.

'Yes.'

'Was Reverend Mother strict?'

'She was nice.' Beatrice shrugged. 'She knew every-thing—well, we thought she did.'

'Were the other nuns strict?'

'Sister Josephine had it in for Alicia.' She looked up. 'Thankfully, I left before Alicia hit puberty...'

Please leave it, she begged. Her cold, cold heart was slowly filling up and she didn't know what to do about it. *Please hurry up in there...*

'You left...?' he asked.

'I got a scholarship. Languages.' She revealed nothing that wasn't on her résumé, but she did add a slight personal touch. 'I loved Latin.'

'Yuck,' Julius said. 'Were you the teacher's pet?'

'Sister Catherine didn't have favourites.'

The feeling in her heart was getting painful now, and she wished he would stop.

'I can find you a word game on my tablet if you're bored...'

'I'm not bored. Just curious. Taylor...' he mused. 'That doesn't sound very Italian.'

'No.'

'What would that be in Sicilian?' Julius thought for a moment. 'Tagghiari?' he offered. 'Or Sarto?' He said the Italian word for tailor and when she still gave no response, he moved on. 'So, your parents...?'

'I really don't discuss my private life, sir.'

'No, you don't, do you?' Julius said. 'Yet you get a front row seat to mine.'

'It's my job,' she retorted, simultaneously regretting her standoffish tone. It was what she was always like. Not just with Julius, but with everyone.

It wasn't working today, though.

Despite what he'd said at the interview, it *was* a game,

Beatrice realised. Just not one she'd thought she'd ever play. It was a grown-up game, and the exchanges were little slivers of personal information. Tiny pieces that built up with each little reveal—and her pile was building.

Memories.

Opinions.

Private thoughts.

Despite her constraints, each day he brought a little more of himself to the table, and she scooped it up while putting little down herself.

Yet, she'd just told him about Alicia, and that felt like an awful lot.

'Sir…'

He shook his head and got to his feet. 'Here we go.'

'I apologise for keeping you waiting, Your Highness.' Phillipe, Head of Palace Protocol welcomed the Prince. 'Everything is in place.'

There was a table of grim faces, and the men all stood as they entered. Beatrice took her place amongst them and looked down at the folder containing the agenda, waiting for Julius to take his seat so she could read it…

But Julius did not take a seat.

'Sir?' Phillipe motioned to a chair. 'Again, I apologise for the delay. There was rather a lot to get through.'

'Then you'll be pleased to know that this won't take long,' Julius said. 'Don't ever keep me waiting again.'

So it wasn't the prospect of his bridal selection that had been winding him up; it was far more straightforward than that—and now he let them know exactly what he thought.

'I have taken on the workload of my late brother, my sister, who is raising a young family, as well as my mother, your Queen, who is deeply grieving.' He picked up the agenda and tore it up. 'I'm going abroad at dawn on Friday, and yet you think I have time to sit out there—'

'Sir,' Phillipe was brave enough to interrupt. 'These pictures need to be addressed. They are rather—'

'I suggest you stop there,' Julius said, and thankfully Phillipe took that advice and snapped his mouth closed.

'What was your King doing that night? Or your Queen? Do they have to report their actions?'

An aide to the King spoke then. 'The King knows how upset his people are—'

'Bring me one of them,' he challenged. 'There are no baying mobs out there. Know this: I celebrate my brother's life and I mourn his passing, and how I do that is my choice.'

He clearly did not need Beatrice there to hold his hand.

'There's your response,' he said, and threw her bland words on the table. 'Don't you get that every time you apologise for me you undermine my future reign? And whoever put the possibility of rehab on the table would have been marched out through the door if they were working in *my* household.'

He looked at every person in turn, marking their cards. They all looked suitably awkward and not all were able to meet his eyes.

'Don't forget—sooner or later I *shall* be King.'

He swept out, and Beatrice quickly gathered up her bag and papers, but as she stepped into the Great Hall, she halted—for Queen Teiria stood there.

She was a striking woman.

Always had been and always would be.

Today she wore a red velvet robe, and a headdress with tiny jewelled coins on it. She had passed on her beautiful black almond-shaped eyes to her children, Beatrice noted.

'Julius.'

She didn't even glance in Beatrice's direction. She was

there to speak with her son. He suggested they take a walk, or have a late-afternoon tea.

'I don't want tea, Julius.' She stared up at him. 'You do know a king has to put duty above all else?'

Beatrice stood back, her head down, awaiting Julius's smart retort—perhaps pointing out that he wasn't yet King, or that he was currently doing the 'duty' of most of his family—but he said nothing.

'You have had so much leeway, Julius. I have fought for that—just as I have fought for all my children. It's time to remember the promise you made.'

Beatrice looked up and she saw that the usually very confident heir's complexion was tinged grey.

'I have never been more serious, Julius.'

Suddenly, so too was the Prince.

There was no witty retort, no shrug, just silence.

It was Queen Teiria who broke it. 'No more delays.'

She swept off, and of course Julius offered no explanation to Beatrice. He seemed to have forgotten she was there.

But then suddenly he turned. 'Thank you,' he told her. 'I won't be needing you for the rest of the day.'

Dismissed.

CHAPTER FIVE

WHAT PROMISE HAD been made?

Beatrice called Jordan on her way back, as arranged.

'I heard,' Jordan said, by way of greeting.

Beatrice wasn't sure if she was talking about Julius's meeting with the aides or what the Queen had said. 'Well, I'm just letting you know.'

'Thank you,' Jordan said.

They spoke about the press response, and also the need for a lovely, wholesome picture of their prince.

'Can I have access to his diary?' Beatrice asked as she arrived back in her office. 'I want to sort out an interview and photoshoot, and I want to see the rest of the anniversary photos and footage myself.'

'You'll have to come up.'

Beatrice held in a sigh. She needed the computers upstairs to access his diary, even though she could only type in requests which Jordan had to approve. The passage and stairs to Julius's private offices and residence were seriously starting to irk her, but reminding herself it was just for a few more weeks she started the trek.

And then halted midway.

Only three weeks left. And he would be away for one of them.

In truth, it wasn't the stairs nor the limited access that frustrated her now.

Nor even the fact that Julius drifted into her office from his residence on occasion—or, worse, stood there all gleaming and reeking of cologne on his way out.

It was simply that in three weeks she'd be gone.

It was strange to stand on a staircase and realise that for the first time ever she felt a little at home.

It wasn't just him. It was the islands, the people, the palace, her little flat and balcony. How she was starting to know the people on the bus, and how the barista remembered her order.

Jordan, Tobias, even gossipy Despina... All of them were starting to feel like colleagues rather than people who happened to work where she had landed temporarily.

The odd staffer at her last job might have remembered to ask if she wanted to come for a drink once or twice, but here everyone was waiting to hear Tobias's news—Beatrice included...

Stop it.

She took the last steps and found Jordan in a foul mood—so that helped Beatrice feel better about soon leaving the palace! She practically hammered a limited access code into one of the computers for her.

Good.

And no Julius.

Extra-good!

'Are you going to be at the Flower Festival the Saturday after next?' Jordan asked in a grumpy voice.

'No,' Beatrice said.

Jordan ignored her. 'It's a strict dress code,' she informed her.

'For a flower festival?'

'No, to get into the royal marquee,' Jordan said. 'You

can bring a guest—just make sure they know about the dress code.'

'I'm not really big on festivals.'

'Beatrice, all the staff will be there,' Jordan pushed. 'I'm going to try and get there.'

'You only fly in that morning,' Beatrice pointed out. 'Surely you'll be exhausted?'

'A little… But Princess Jasmine is the royal patron and it would be nice to give her some support.'

Beatrice was tight-lipped. Perhaps if the rules weren't so rigid here then it would be Princess Jasmine who was off to Oman and South East Asia, rather than giving a speech at a flower festival.

That wasn't really what was upsetting Beatrice, though. It was the fact that she was starting to be invited to things, yet soon she'd be gone.

'Beatrice, I know you're a temp, but it would be nice if you could make *some* effort to be sociable.'

Beatrice gritted her teeth and resisted reminding Jordan that they weren't all devoted to the palace. That it was their prince's being so actively 'sociable' that was causing all their headaches right now.

'Beatrice…' Jordan spoke more nicely now. 'I really think you should try and get there. Honestly, the colours…'

'What colours?'

Beatrice stiffened at the sound of his voice.

He invited himself into any conversation with such ease! How did he do that?

'I'm trying to get Beatrice to join us at the Flower Festival.'

'Don't do it.' He shook his head. 'Not with your allergies.'

Jordan changed the subject. 'Beatrice wants you to do a photoshoot in the stables.'

'No,' he flatly refused.

'It's a really good journalist,' Beatrice said, 'and I think—'

He ignored her and took a bottle of Limoncello from a small freezer.

Jordan gave a nod. 'Just a small one.'

'Beatrice?' he politely offered.

'No, thank you.'

His grey tinge had gone and there was no trace of the storm that had hit him this afternoon. He didn't have a Limoncello either, but poured one for Jordan, and then the two of them went and sat on their oh-so-cosy seats and went through his schedule for the upcoming trip as Beatrice tried not to listen.

'You'll need a gift for the daughter,' Jordan said.

'Oh, no.' He shook his head. 'I'm serious. Otherwise I'll end up with two brides.'

Apparently there was a poem he had to learn in Romeyka, and, no, he hadn't managed to look at it yet.

Actually, it all sounded completely exhausting, Beatrice thought, watching footage of the family on the balcony after Claude's funeral as she tried not to listen in. A night in his mother's hometown, then two nights in Oman, and then on to South East Asia and then back—all in the space of a week.

'Back in time for the Flower Festival,' Jordan said to him, although Beatrice rather felt it was aimed at her.

'Please…' he scoffed, and Beatrice found she was suppressing a smile. 'I'll be in no mood for company by then.'

Diary closed, Jordan stood. 'Have you heard from Tobias, sir?'

'I have,' Julius said. 'How about you?'

'Yes,' Jordan said. 'I've been sworn to silence.'

'And me.'

Ha-ha-ha…

They shared their little laugh and Beatrice wanted to poke out her tongue at their friendliness as Jordan said goodbye to him. Instead, she turned back to her video and watched as the royal family all walked back into the palace from the balcony, the King reaching for his wife's hand and her brushing it off.

Whoa!

Beatrice rewound.

Oh, yes, she had!

'I'll see you tomorrow, sir,' Jordan said.

'No doubt.'

'Oh, before I go…' Jordan stopped. 'No. It's nothing.'

'You know I hate that,' Julius said. 'Say what you were going to say.'

'Very well. Have you got that book?'

'Book?'

'The one I lent you.'

'Oh, I thought it was a gift.'

Beatrice found herself looking over, enjoying the very rare sight of Julius squirming.

'No,' Jordan said. 'I told you it was a loan.'

'I'll get on to it.'

'You haven't read it, have you?' Jordan said. 'Sir…?'

'Jordan, I *have* read it.' He must also have seen her disbelief. 'I have—along with all your endless and very personal notes in the margins. We used to get fined if we did that at school.'

She smiled. 'You've never paid a fine in your life, sir.'

'I'm just letting you know that I did read it.'

'Did it help?'

'It did—thank you. I'll get it back to you.'

He pulled a face when she'd safely gone, and swore under his breath, but then he must have remembered that Beatrice was there and he half turned his head.

'She keeps asking for it.'

'Oh?'

'I think I might have tossed it into the ocean.'

'You threw her book into the sea?'

'It annoyed me.' He took out his phone and called Tobias, asking him to call the staff on his yacht to have another look for it. 'Honestly, never lend me a book.'

'I won't. What was it about?'

'It was a patronising book on grief.' He rolled his eyes and then came over and perched on her desk. 'What are you watching?'

'Footage of Claude's funeral and of the one-year anniversary memorial service,' Beatrice said. 'Your behaviour was impeccable.'

'Thank you.'

'So this book you borrowed and lost…?'

'It was awful. As well as that there were all the notes Jordan had made in the margins. Believe me, I'm not going to go into detail, but it felt like I was reading her diary.'

'She's very—' Beatrice stopped. She herself might be cold and friendless, but she didn't gossip.

Julius smiled. 'If she talks too much then it means she likes you. She's so indiscreet—but only in here. Anyway,' he added, 'I don't think her magical book applied to me…'

'Because you're unique?'

'Actually, yes.' He gave her another smile. 'It said that I'm to "talk about the departed",' he quoted. 'But every time I do they all bow and lower their eyes.'

'Oh.'

'You don't, though,' he said. 'Honestly, that's probably why I caved.'

'Caved?'

He nodded.

'What else did the book say?'

'That I should try not to make major changes or big decisions for a year. Well, that wasn't going to be possible. I immediately became the heir. I was hauled back here, given more staff…'

He was right.

'What else?' she asked.

'That I should let people know how I'm feeling.' His smile was tight.

Beatrice, whose social skills were so dire she couldn't even manage the thought of a flower festival, would usually have given an equally tight smile in response, closed down the computer and wished him goodnight, but instead she took a breath.

'You can,' she offered.

'Please…' He rolled his eyes at her offer.

How rude! He hadn't even noticed that she was trying to be nice.

'So, I threw the book in the sea.'

'Get her a new one.'

'Should I?'

'Say you made a lot of notes in her copy and underlined some bits. Perhaps say something about privacy…'

'Yes!' He was delighted by her solution. 'Could you do that now, please?'

'I'm not your PA.'

'No, but it's *for* my PA.'

He smiled as he got his way and her fingers typed out the search and purchase of a new book for Jordan.

'Done,' Beatrice said, and told him how much he owed her.

'I don't carry cash.'

'Transfer it, then.'

'I'll call Tobias and ask him.'

'Leave him alone.' Beatrice actually laughed. 'Oh, my God, you're…'

She didn't know what. Incorrigible? Annoying? Spoilt? She tried all of those words, but as she reached for her bag it was other words that sprang to her mind, and they should *not* be springing to her mind—at least not with him so close.

He moved away from the desk, thank goodness, and went to the decanter to pour a whisky for himself, as he sometimes did.

'Do you want one?' he asked, as if suddenly remembering his manners.

'No,' Beatrice said. 'I mean, no, thank you. Sir.'

They were in his office now.

And, despite the polite refusal, she very much did want one. It felt like a whisky kind of night.

Whatever that meant.

'Are you sure?' he checked.

'Quite sure. I had one too many Birthday Girl Martinis at the weekend—' She tried to make a joke, but he cut it off at the neck.

'Beatrice, can we stop with the hay fever and hangover excuses? We both know you'd been crying when you came in this morning.' When she neither confirmed nor denied it, he made his point. 'So—no, thank you, to your offer to hear how I'm feeling. Clearly it's a one-way offer!'

'That's unfair.'

'Is it?' He looked at her, and there was no repentance, no apology or taking it back. 'Okay, if we're going to talk, why don't you go first? Why were you upset this morning?'

She sat there and didn't speak. Couldn't speak.

'Okay, let's start with an easier one: how was your weekend?'

Beatrice said nothing.

'So I was right. You don't actually want conversation?'

She did.

Badly.

So badly that finally she nodded.

'The friend I was telling you about this morning...' She raked a hand through her hair. 'We lost touch. Completely my fault.'

'Fault?'

'My choice,' Beatrice said. 'But I know it would have hurt her an awful lot.'

'You were children.'

'It would still have hurt.'

It was too hard to explain to him that she'd changed her surname just to survive, and that in doing so had effectively cut off any chance of Alicia finding and contacting her. Nor could she tell him how essential a completely new start had felt at the time.

'This weekend I went back to Trebordi for the first time in a decade. I was hoping to find out what had happened to her.'

'No luck?'

'In truth, when I got there... I didn't actually try. I realised it's perhaps best left...' She shook her head, and for a moment it felt as if the day that had started in tears might end the same way. 'Really...' Beatrice nodded a little urgently '...it's best left.'

'Okay.'

He said it kindly.

Patiently.

She met his eyes and he gave a slight nod, as if he understood how hard it had been for her to share, even though she hadn't told him very much.

So hard.

The silence between them felt like an invitation to say more. But Beatrice dared not, or she really would cry, and so she did what she did best and deflected the conversation back to him.

'I think it might be my turn to ask a question.'

'I walked into that,' Julius admitted, then gave a short, rueful laugh. 'Go ahead,' he said. 'I think…'

Beatrice swallowed, and as she did so tasted the salty tears she'd been holding in at the back of her throat. Julius held her gaze and she found she had just one question: she wanted to ask if the eyes that held hers really were laced with desire. She wanted to know whether, if she dared to stand up and walk over to him now, he would reach for her and hold her…just for a moment. And then, after that moment, would she be allowed to give in and stop battling desire? Or was she crazy to be thinking such things?

That was her question.

Quite a long question.

She left quite a long pause as she considered asking it. And yet the whole time his eyes never left her face as she fought to be brave and voice it.

Come on, Beatrice, his eyes seemed to say.

Nothing moved. Even the hands on his watch had surely stopped, for there was not a sound she could hear—not even her breathing. So sure was she, when held by his gaze, that she almost risked asking it.

It was her own mocking voice that hauled her back. The voice in her head that reminded her of her complete inexperience and the agony of his brush-off if she was reading this wrong.

Rejection.

Oh, God.

She was terrified of it.

In *every* area of her life.

And so she blinked, hauled herself back from the dangerous edge, and searched the thick air for a question.

'What promise?'

'Sorry?'

He frowned, and then his mouth opened in a smile so incredulous, so confused, that she wondered if he'd misheard her.

'What promise was your mother referring to—?'

Even though the lights hadn't been off, it felt as if they'd suddenly come back on. Whatever spell had been cast was now broken.

'You *know* I can't answer that.'

Beatrice couldn't quite believe she had asked. Except it still felt safer than the other question.

She'd been about to step forward and attempt to kiss that angry mouth, Beatrice thought in horror. She'd been about to reveal her deep desire.

And so, rather than back-pedal, she snapped, 'Then it's *you* who doesn't want conversation,' Beatrice told him. 'Sir!'

She felt a little giddy as she walked over to Jordan's desk. She felt a curious mixture of anger, towards herself for confiding in him, horror at how close she had come to lowering her guard, and embarrassment at such an inappropriate question.

And she was determined to get back on track.

She flicked off the computer and commenced packing her bag, as she always did. She paused and looked over briefly. 'I answered the question you asked. You, sir, did not.'

Julius watched her, not in the least chastised.

Clearly she was feeling vindicated as she packed up her bag, and he tried to recall when it had first annoyed him.

Diary: close. Pen: put it in a box. Computer: put into its case. *Zip. Snap, snap, snap.* Whether in her office, or his, whether in a meeting room or sitting by the lake, Beatrice kept her possessions with her at all times. She was like a speedy little tortoise, carrying everything on her person, ready to disappear into herself or vanish without trace, leaving nothing of herself.

Well, she'd left *something*—but a tale of a long-lost friend didn't come close to what she was really asking him to share.

Was Beatrice stupid or did she really not know the basic rules of engagement? Seriously?

He asked himself the question again, already knowing for certain it wasn't the former.

Off she stomped, her bag on her shoulder. The woman who had put everyone's backs up. The woman who preferred to eat her lunch by the lake alone. The woman who shut down all attempts by her colleagues to be friendly.

She *didn't* know, Julius realised. Oh, she could handle the press, and cut down his aides with few words, and she was brilliant to go into a hostile room with.

But Beatrice did not know the basic rules of engagement. She hadn't even known what to do with a birthday cake!

He couldn't understand it, nor even explain it, but in that moment it suddenly dawned on him that she actually didn't know the rules. And he wasn't thinking about palace protocol, or anything as complex as that.

She didn't know the basics.

'Beatrice.'

He was still irritated by her question, yet he was no longer angry—not even when she chose to ignore him and marched furiously out of the room and down the corridor.

'Beatrice.' He caught up with her just before she got out of sight. 'Wait.'

'For what?' She turned.

'We were talking…'

'No.' She shook her head. 'We weren't. I'll hand in my questions next time in advance, for your approval.'

He tried not to smile, and had to bite his lower lip to stop himself. How should he handle this liaison aide, who was actually dreadful at communication?

'Beatrice…' he was almost out of breath '…you don't go straight for the jugular.'

'What?'

'When you want to know something about another person—something awkward, or difficult, or personal—you don't go straight for the jugular.'

'I told you about my friend.'

'You did,' Julius agreed.

He knew he was on the right path.

'But I could tell when you'd said enough. I respected the fact that you'd told me it was best left. I knew there was more—of course there's more—but you asked that it be left so I didn't wade in with more questions.'

Yes, he was definitely on the right path because her nostrils pinched.

'I pulled back…' he said.

She swallowed.

'We're not in a meeting, Beatrice. You don't have to go straight in for the kill.'

His words were starting to seep in, and the worst part was, Beatrice knew he was right.

He wasn't completely right, because he didn't know just how big a part of her heart she'd shared, but her question had been beyond inappropriate. She screwed her eyes closed in bitter recall as she replayed her own words.

'Got it?' he asked, but kindly.

She nodded, took a breath, opened her eyes and nodded again. 'Got it. Be more subtle next time.'

He laughed a one-burst laugh and she felt it on her cheek. 'You still wouldn't have got an answer.'

His eyes widened at the very thought, as though there was no one—not a soul—who could have asked him that and received an answer. She had everyone's backs up, yet somehow, not his.

Never his.

He liked the distance she kept.

He liked how it amplified things when they were close.

They were—despite their half-row, despite her walking off, despite so little having been revealed—somehow closer than before.

In fact, if there was anyone he could tell his secrets, then he'd probably choose the woman staring back at him now.

He'd been waiting for her kiss a few moments ago... wanting to take her to bed and end this frustration.

Now there was a new craving.

The desire to take her to bed was not new, but far more dangerous was the desire to know her, and for her to know him better too.

He stepped back. 'I'll say goodnight.'

'Goodnight. Sir.'

'Best left,' he said, and returned to his office and closed the door behind him.

She carried on down the stairs when all she wished was that she were back there... Wished she'd been more subtle.

Yet Julius had just revealed something.

He had said she'd gone straight for the kill. And that told her that whatever promise had been made it was his agony to bear it.

She walked towards Prince's Lane, caught the shuttle

bus, and tried to make sense of things as the bus hissed its way through town. Only when she got home did she remember to turn off her work phone.

Except she checked the messages first.

Not for work, but just in case there might be a message from him.

It wasn't so much that something had shifted—it was more as if something had been revealed. A tiny fault in the heavy veil between them had been exposed…a little glimmer of a light…a star that had always been there but which had previously been unseen. That was how it felt.

Not as though she was standing behind a stage curtain, peering out, more that she was sitting on the other side of the curtain and had suddenly glimpsed a scintilla of the Julius behind the royal veneer.

One, two, three… Like stars in the night sky things emerged, and she was entranced by them, far too aware.

Until the veil between them was dotted with stars—well, for Beatrice at least.

And even if she'd messed up back there, it had been worth it.

She didn't know how to describe it.

She only knew that it really felt as if it could have been a whisky kind of night.

Whatever that was…

CHAPTER SIX

STARRY NIGHTS FADED, THOUGH, and pink clouds were fleeting when you worked for Julius.

Beatrice happily hid in her office for most of the following week.

There were not many drop-ins from the dashing Prince.

He was busy doing fly-in, fly-out visits to a couple of the smaller islands and so was barely around, and even when he was, he was vague and polite.

Thoughts of that odd encounter—the kiss that had never happened and the almost-row—dispersed as Beatrice got through the week.

And it was quite a difficult week in the end, because the dancing-on-a-boat shots hadn't just lit a twinkle in Beatrice's knickers…there was glitter everywhere she looked!

Everyone, it seemed, had a story, or a photo, and Beatrice spent most of her time playing whack-a-mole with all the reports and counter-reports that has been generated, trying to keep her newly wholesome prince's image intact.

On Friday, she had no choice but to go up to his offices and access the computers, and get Jordan reluctantly to let her into the archives.

'I don't have time for this,' Jordan muttered, typing in a code for her. 'I finish at two…'

'I know.'

'It's not you,' she said. 'It's this damn "Dancing King" thing. He's been invited onto a ballroom dancing TV show...'

'He's not going to do it?' Beatrice gaped.

'God knows! Can you believe the King actually called him this morning to discuss it?'

This place!

Beatrice was cross-eyed from cross-referencing the Prince's exes as lunchtime approached.

'Who's the Marchioness?' she asked.

'Oh, my God!' Jordan gave a dramatic wince, 'Don't ask.'

Beatrice did as she was told and didn't!

Not that it stopped Jordan from telling her. 'She was seriously connected. I mean, real hetaera material...'

'A long-term mistress before marriage?'

'Oh, yes, it happens all the time. Anyway, she was newly widowed after having nursed her husband for years. There was no mourning period for the Marchioness—she wanted soirées...'

Beatrice rather guessed she was looking at Julius's one-on-one Latin American dance tutor.

'Well, at least he's behaving now.'

'He's being discreet, you mean.'

Unlike you, his PA, Beatrice was tempted to point out. Yet she was coming to quite like their chats.

'I'm quite sure Prince's Lane resembles Grand Central Station at times,' Jordan went on.

Or she *had* been starting to like their chats!

'Sorry?'

'Just before the stables...where the shuttle bus drops his staff off.'

'I know where it is.' Beatrice bristled.

'Well, there are special gates…' She lowered her voice. 'There's a tunnel that runs under Prince's Lane.'

'Why wasn't I told this?'

'Nobody's "told". It's just a piece of knowledge you acquire if you work here long enough.' She laughed. 'You haven't seen anything?'

'What?'

'I used to think the place was haunted by beautiful women in ball gowns, walking through the mist.'

'Are you saying that he has a secret passage to his suite?'

'Beatrice!' Jordan frowned at the clear annoyance in the usually unruffled liaison aide. 'He's not the only one; it's like a rabbit warren beneath here.'

Of course it was. Beatrice took a short-cut sometimes through one of those passages, if she was running late, and the morning coffee came via another… But a direct passage to his suite? No wonder he was so cocksure about 'behaving'.

She felt a fire burning in her chest and had to fight to prevent the heat rising to her cheeks. 'Well, it would have been nice to have been warned.'

But she had been…sort of. Now she looked back on it. It was in her job description, Beatrice reminded herself.

'Shh…' Jordan said, as the buzzer lit up to indicate that he'd left his apartment.

At least you got a slight warning of his approach when you were up here in Jordan's office.

Beatrice carried on working as he sauntered past.

'Ah, the Marchioness,' he said fondly as he looked over her shoulder.

'They're saying…' Beatrice wished he would get away from her shoulder '…that you broke up with her because she was past childbearing age.'

'Are they, now?' He shrugged and offered no insight. None at all.

'You are discreet—I'll give you that.' Beatrice turned her head just a bit and smiled, then got back to looking at the screen. 'Even I don't really know what you get up to.'

'As it should be,' he said.

'So, no further response?'

'Of course not.'

She clicked away from the image of the Marchioness and a much younger Prince Julius with marked relief— only it was short-lived, because he came beside her and leant on the desk.

'They're just going to keep digging...' he said.

'Well, you're giving them nothing new.' She looked up a little, and knew that she too was digging. 'Unless there is something...?'

'Sorry?'

'Well, if there is it's best we get ahead of it.'

He didn't respond. Instead he started to talk to Jordan about their crack-of-dawn departure the following morning. Except even though he was ignoring her question Beatrice couldn't ignore him. Julius's thigh was in her periphery, and his hand still held her desk, and she *couldn't* ignore that.

Thank goodness he flew out tomorrow, or she might just have to walk out on her job today.

This minute, in fact.

She wanted to nudge his fingers, to let him know her hand was close and feel the bliss of his hand closing over hers for a second...a squeeze of acknowledgement, saying that he *knew*, that they were both aware of each other, even as they did nothing, even as he chatted away...

'I might go and have lunch,' Beatrice said, and started to pack up her things.

'Leave all that,' Jordan said. 'I need you up here this afternoon. Anyway, lunch is being catered today. Tobias is doing the gender reveal…'

'Why?' Julius frowned. 'We already know it's a boy.'

'He's not expecting you to be there,' Jordan said. 'It's just us that have to act surprised.'

'We all know, though.'

'Just…' Jordan was cross. 'Have lunch with us all, Beatrice.'

'I actually brought my own in,' Beatrice said. 'I might get some air.'

Snap, close, zip.

Julius saw Jordan's eyes close in frustration at Beatrice's refusal to join in, and then open wide as Beatrice took herself off for lunch.

'See?' Jordan hissed. 'Why even try to include her?'

Julius didn't respond. Normally he didn't get involved in office politics, but where Beatrice was concerned…

'Are you going to speak with her, sir?'

'About…?'

'Well, I can't offer her a permanent role without telling her what it entails.'

'Be vague.'

'That won't wash with Beatrice,' Jordan warned. 'You know her contract expires in two weeks. She's already fielding approaches.'

'Who from?'

'I don't know. She closes her door, or goes to the lake…' She walked over to a window. 'She's on her phone now.'

'You said you had reservations,' Julius reminded her.

'Some,' Jordan admitted. 'Though they're nothing I can't address with Beatrice myself. It's your call, sir.'

He nodded.

'I'm going to pop down to the staffroom. You do remember I'm finishing at two…?'

'Yes, I'll see you at dawn.'

'I'll be here long before then. Sir, if you want me to squeeze in a formal interview with Beatrice before I leave…?'

He'd better speak with Beatrice now.

And say what?

Beatrice, you are brilliant at your job, and I can think of no one better to deal with the barrage from the press when I sign the Document of intent. However, I need you to leave so I can sign said document. And can we have one night together as a reward for good behaviour after your leaving do?

Hardly.

He glanced down and there Beatrice was, alone by the lake rather than eating blue cupcakes with her colleagues. There was a forlorn air to her that tripped some unknown switch buried within him.

She was making friends—not that she knew it yet. His close-knit team were warming to her. Jordan had even negotiated on Beatrice's behalf, prior to any offer, insisting on an attractive package in order to convince her to stay.

She would, as Jordan said, be an asset to the team.

The moral dilemma was all his.

He took the stairs with purpose, crossed the terrace with elegant ease, then slowed as he approached the lake.

'Oh.' She turned at his footsteps and went to stand up. 'Excuse me…'

'Don't get up,' he said. 'Do you mind if I join you?'

'Of course not,' she said, but he could hear her reluctance at having him invade her oh-so-personal space.

He peered into her very neat lunchbox, and then at

Beatrice. He was good at this, Julius reminded himself. Small talk. Job offer. Small talk.

'You like to take lunch here?' he asked.

'I like the peace.' Beatrice nodded. 'Well…'

'Sorry to intrude.'

She actually laughed, and it was a sound so unfamiliar to him that it seemed like windchimes above them. Usually windchimes annoyed him, but not this sunny afternoon.

'That came out wrong,' Beatrice admitted, and even managed another small laugh. 'The peacocks are really noisy today.'

'Ah…' he nodded. 'Bastards.'

She turned, startled.

'They screech me awake an hour before my alarm.' Small talk was so easy. 'If I set it for five, they rise at four. If I set it for seven, they wake at six…' He glanced over. Enough small talk? Perhaps a moment longer…? 'You feed the swans?' he asked.

'The black ones.' She nodded. 'They're all fledging except that one.' She pointed to the straggler. 'He's lazy,' Beatrice said, watching as he hopped onto a little island of rushes and started calling out as his family glided off. 'He still likes to hitch a ride on his mother's back. She always goes back for him.'

'It's natural.'

'No!' Beatrice disputed. 'He should be independent by now. Cats are the same—they have nothing to do with their kittens after a few months.'

Julius took a breath. He was not here for her depressing take on Mother Nature. 'Beatrice, you know I fly out for a week in the morning?'

'Yes.'

'You're aware, I'm sure, that initially I didn't want to hire you.'

'You made that very clear.'

'Well, I was wrong. You have been a great help.' He looked over at her pressed lips and pointed little nose. 'I sincerely mean that. You've taken a lot of the pressure off my dealings with the press and the aides—all of it, really. However...'

'Am I being fired?'

'No!' He shook his head. 'We wouldn't be sitting by the lake if that were the case. But your contract is due to expire soon.'

'Two weeks today,' Beatrice said.

She was counting the days. Dreading that final day. But also relieved that soon this slow torment would end.

Her desire had become a perpetual thing. It woke her in the night and it morphed into her dreams, and then it was intensified by day until she could not escape it.

Not even by the lake.

No, for today he'd come and sat beside her.

They saw the mother swan hiding behind the rushes as the lazy cygnet peeped loudly. They both watched as his mother tried to ignore him.

'What if he isn't strong enough?' Julius asked.

Beatrice shrugged. 'Survival of the fittest.'

'Remind me never to watch a nature documentary with you.'

She half laughed, but it faded when he asked another question—or possibly it was the serious edge to his voice that alerted her.

'What if he can't make it in the deep water?'

Beatrice turned and looked into his dark eyes and she felt as if he was asking her something. Or telling her something. Quite what, she didn't know, but it felt like an extension of their previous exchange.

Be subtle, he'd told her.

No, she corrected herself. He'd told her not to push. To tread gently if there was something awkward or difficult to discuss.

Was this related to the mysterious promise he had made?

Before, she would have frowned and asked exactly that. Now, she sat by his side and tried a different approach.

'Then he stays in the shallows, maybe?' she suggested.

'Or she still carries him,' Julius said, and they turned and watched as the mother swan relented and the little cygnet jumped onto her back.

It felt like a very important conversation.

The leaves were shimmering and the lake was rippling in the breeze, while underneath it all she was trying to understand what was actually being communicated.

'Well, for as long as she can,' Beatrice said. They sat in silence. Then, 'Perhaps I should stop giving him extra corn.'

'Beatrice, when I get back from this trip...'

He didn't actually say it, but she knew where this was leading. It was the point of her being here, after all.

She prepared her smile—a big one—and told it to wait in the wings and be ready to dash on as soon as it was required. She had been working diligently towards this moment, attempting to get this leopard to change his spots, albeit temporarily. And she'd done a good job—an excellent job, in fact.

But the smile she'd prepared must have stage fright, because it refused to leave the wings as he spoke on.

'Things are going to get rather busy...'

'You're not doing that dancing show?'

'No, although believe it or not the King is considering it—to show how progressive and modern the monarchy is.'

She gave him a look that said she begged to differ.

'Well, that's his latest turn of phrase.'

'I'll vote for you,' she told him.

'Thank you,' he said. 'I think. However, it's not that type of busy I'm talking about. My father and I are both in agreement that it's time to steer the country into happier times…'

'I see.'

'Only my very inner circle are aware.'

'Of course.'

'However, the reason I'm letting *you* know is because Jordan is going to offer you a permanent role.'

She swallowed.

'We've discussed it. She's very impressed with your work. She does have a couple of reservations, but you two can sort those out…'

'What reservations?'

'I don't get involved in all that.'

'What reservations does Jordan have?'

'I can't begin to imagine.' He smiled a black smile. 'So, I am formally inviting you…' He made a little circular motion with his hands.

'What does *that* mean?' Beatrice asked, and circled her own hand.

'That I'm extending an invitation for you to become a permanent member of my team and now it's between you and Jordan.' He stood. 'I'll leave you to enjoy your lunch.'

'Thank you,' Beatrice said, a little stunned.

She was about to halt him…to tell him no…to just…

Why halt him?

Why decline?

This was a job in a place she could actually call home, and if she didn't have this ridiculous crush then, yes, she'd seriously consider staying.

She really had averted disaster by not attempting to

kiss him. If he felt so little for her that he could hire her to deal with his wedding then clearly it was all in her head.

Anyway, he was arrogant, haughty, and just so not her type.

Not that she had a type. But if she did it would not be him. Nor any man who opposed women in royal lineage. Nor a man who…

What else?

A man who pointed his finger.

But surely she should at least listen to what Jordan had to say?

Maybe it was time for a different approach.

'I wasn't expecting to be asked…' She looked up and pushed out that smile, but had to squint a little at the sun behind him. 'I'm thrilled.'

Beatrice couldn't see his reaction because of the blinding light. She just saw his shoulders stiffen and guessed the suave Prince might be a little startled by her rare expression of enthusiasm.

'I'm flattered. Thank you, sir.'

CHAPTER SEVEN

TOBIAS WAS IN her office when she returned.

'Everything okay?' Beatrice frowned.

'I was just leaving you a cupcake,' he said. 'I know you couldn't get there, but...' He smiled. 'We're having a boy.'

'Wow!' Beatrice said.

Actually, *wow!*

His excitement was catching, and Beatrice found herself smiling as he showed her a photograph of the scan and spoke about Esther. 'She'll be at the Flower Festival...' he told her.

'Will you?' she asked.

'No chance. We don't get in till ten that morning and I'll be crashing.' He shook his head. 'But if you want company, Esther would love to meet you.'

He was kind.

They were all kind here.

And when Jordan called her upstairs a short time later Beatrice listened carefully to all that was being offered to her, amazed at the benefits package they had put together in order to tempt her to accept the permanent role.

Her choice of press officer, her own assistant, a driver to and from work and the salary... Well, she might even be able to afford the mortgage on a teeny cupboard on the marina...though not one with a balcony.

In her head she was actually thinking of marina views and weekends and coffee shops and being here!

'Now,' Jordan said, 'we have a lot to discuss.'

Yes, there was always room for negotiation. Maybe she could get that balcony after all!

But Jordan wasn't all smiles and waving a contract. 'Beatrice, before we go any further I might ask Deborah from HR to come and join us.'

'HR?'

'Well, I don't want to have to stipulate the number of events you attend, or how you present yourself—'

Beatrice frowned, and then looked down at her immaculate grey shift dress and neat flats and knew she presented herself professionally at all times. 'Do I get a wardrobe allowance for official functions? If there's a dress code...'

'Dress codes are the easy part—it's the social aspect.'

Yikes.

'I don't want to tell you to show up voluntarily and smiling...' Jordan shuddered. This was clearly a conversation she knew was necessary but which she was dreading. 'Why don't I call Deborah now?'

Julius had indeed been right.

Beatrice knew her attitude was being challenged.

'Jordan, you don't need to call HR before you speak with me.'

'The royal family is the touchstone of our culture, our calendar...' Jordan closed her eyes and took a breath. 'Take the Flower Festival—it was cancelled last year...'

'I do understand it's especially important this year.'

'It's important every year; it's a part of us as a nation.'

And Beatrice could be one of the *'us'*.

Aside from her feelings.

Were they even relevant here?

Did it even matter? Because clearly the world was carrying on, oblivious to the torch she carried for the Prince.

Perhaps it was time to snuff it out?

Bring forward her thirtieth birthday, maybe?

Make friends.

Say yes to life.

'I'll leave these with you to go through,' Jordan said, and opened up a glossy navy folder that contained the official palace staff brochure along with an awful lot of forms. 'Take your time to go through them and see what's involved. Formal training in palace protocol…' she turned the pages '…enhanced security vetting—that takes a few weeks…'

'I had that in the UK; it's still current.'

'We'll need our own, as well as counterterrorism measures. There's no way around it. You'll be working here upstairs, with full computer access, diaries, travelling with the royal entourage…'

Beatrice had a sudden image of herself at the rear of the royal jet, watching Julius and his bride. Or dressed in her clothing allowance wedding day best, but on the periphery. Stuck in a perpetual crush and never moving on.

Perhaps sometimes she'd get the evening offer of a cosy chair and a Limoncello and go home happy because he'd told her what a good job she'd done that day. Remain just a ridiculous teenager with a crush inside a twenty-nine-year-old body,

Or a forty-year-old body.

Or fifty.

Sixty?

The years would roll on and there they'd stand, both grey, on her retirement, and he'd smile and thank her for all her service, and his children and grandchildren would all be there…

'Beatrice?'

Her breath was tight in her chest as she glimpsed her possible future. One in which she remained safe for ever because she had a crush on the unattainable—which meant she never, ever had to move on.

Beatrice wanted to move on.

That was why she'd gone searching for her friend— for someone who had always understood that, despite her coldness and aloofness, she was hurting.

She was ashamed of having barely searched for Alicia. Of having turned her back on the one person who had ever loved her. Just to survive.

She could hear Jordan's voice, but it sounded as if it was being piped under water... 'We can speak when I'm back. I'm sure you'll have many questions...'

'Actually, no.' Beatrice heard her cold tone and softened it. 'I'm flattered to be asked, but I don't want to waste your time...'

'Beatrice?'

Jordan was looking at the page Beatrice seemed to be fixed on—about security checks. Little did she know that it wasn't the prospect of security checks that had Beatrice about to refuse the job offer. How could she know that it was the thought of being a part of the Prince's entourage that made her hesitate?

'I know already about the name-change. Is it that?'

Beatrice looked at her colleague...her almost new friend.

'It was flagged for a security check.'

'Of course.'

Jordan had Beatrice's file in front of her, which contained a more detailed résumé than the bullet-pointed pages that had been handed to Julius to review. She had probably known all along that Beatrice was a Trebordi baby.

'I just prefer short-term contracts,' Beatrice said. 'It was lovely to be asked, though.'

'You don't want some time to think about it?'

'I don't.'

'I'm very sorry to hear that.'

'Thank you.' Beatrice let out a breath. 'I'm terrible at social things. It's just not for me.' She very deliberately changed the topic. 'What time do you leave?'

'Now,' Jordan said, gathering up all the files. 'Can you stay up here for the afternoon? Everyone who's going on the trip is at home, and Despina finished at one...'

'Sure.'

'I doubt he'll be around,' Jordan said.

Jordan logged out of her secured profile on her computer and left Beatrice with her limited access.

'I'll be in touch all the time. Well, not at the weekend or after five!' Jordan gave a tight smile. 'I know you don't like to be contacted out of work hours.'

'You can contact me on my private line in an emergency.'

'If there's an emergency Beatrice, I doubt I'll be calling you.'

She meant it lightly—meant that a temp wasn't on the list of people to call if something dire occurred. It just hurt, this odd Friday afternoon.

'I'm out of here,' Jordan said.

She had to get her hair done, she said, and pack a suitable wardrobe... She listed off the million things she had to do in order to be back here long before dawn, so Prince Julius could roll out of bed and board the royal jet.

Well, that wasn't fair. Beatrice knew Julius worked harder than anyone she knew—including Jordan, including herself. It was just safer to let her mind linger in its current critical and scathing mode than to indulge in the fantasy that was trying to play out in her head—the one where she had a permanent job at the palace and friends who dropped in for a chat and sat on her balcony...

'I really am going this time,' Jordan said.

There was a rush of regret as Jordan headed off, and Beatrice battled an urge to call her back, to say *To hell with it, yes, I would love to stay.*

She tried to do some work, but kept getting met with 'Limited Access'.

Limited Access.

It felt like the story of her life.

It hurt.

Everything hurt today.

Finally she got into a redacted version of the Prince's diary and did her best not to notice as he came out of his apartment at five.

'Where is everyone?' He frowned.

'Gone for the day.'

'Jordan?'

Beatrice took a breath and held it in, instead of biting back the information that his PA would be back before dawn.

'Oh, yes, of course...' Julius answered himself.

She glanced up at his voice and knew he must have realised, but she tried to hold on to her safe scathing thoughts.

Only it was proving impossible. She was faced with the immaculate Prince, with his freshly cut hair, his nails buffed... Whoever had shaved him had slapped on way too much cologne. No, not quite immaculate, she was faced with the restless Prince. He had removed his jacket and loosened his tie and, presumably because of the hour, his shirt was untucked and he wore no shoes or socks.

He had never looked more incredible than he did right

now. And for a man who always looked amazing, that was saying something.

Even his *feet* were attractive, Beatrice reluctantly noted.

The silence was an uncomfortable one—or was she simply upset? Ready to go home?

These feelings that were currently being squeezed out of the stone that beat in her chest hurt just as much as bottling them all up and ignoring them.

She attempted normality and passed on the messages Jordan had left, and then she got to the last one: 'Queen Teiria has asked that you speak with her before you leave.'

'Done.' He nodded. 'Thank you.'

'Are you packed?' Beatrice attempted to make polite conversation.

'I just have to polish my boots…' he said. 'They really need to shine for Horon tomorrow night.'

'Better get to it, then,' she said, and looked back to her screen. Then she realised she was again a beat too late to catch a joke. 'You're not in there polishing your boots, are you?'

'Correct.'

'Or packing?'

'Nope,' he said, taking the top off the decanter and splashing whisky into a heavy glass.

Julius glanced over to where Beatrice sat at Jordan's desk. Her hair was beginning to fall down, but it looked charmingly dishevelled rather than messy.

There was something else about her that was different too.

Just a slight sense of disarray that he could not articulate.

She wore grey, but that was all she ever wore. As if a

sad cloud hung over her wardrobe, so it produced grey after grey after grey...

No jewellery, as usual.

Her slick of neutral lipstick was in place.

She just looked different.

'Did Jordan speak with you?' he asked.

'Yes.' Beatrice nodded. 'She asked me to work up here for the remainder of the day. If I'm in the way I can move down to my own office—'

'I meant,' he interrupted tartly, 'did she speak to you about coming on board?'

He added ice to his whisky, heard two chinks as the cubes clattered into his glass. He did not offer her one tonight.

'She did.' Beatrice looked back to the screen. 'I really think you should do this interview. Just puppies and ponies—'

'What interview?'

'I told you about it last week. You agreed.'

'Why would I when I don't have any puppies and I grew out of ponies more than twenty years ago?'

'It's for your new wholesome image.'

Julius did not want to discuss puppies or ponies. He wanted to know what his sullen, moody liaison aide was thinking.

'So, did Jordan speak with you?' he prompted. 'About the permanent role?'

'Oh, yes.'

Beatrice thought for a moment, and it was then that she realised there really were some advantages to keeping her private life so very private.

'There's a lot to think about—and obviously I'm going to have to discuss it with my partner.'

It felt as if a whip had just been cracked—as if the air had been sliced open. And she was the one holding the whip.

Beatrice watched Julius arch his neck, as he did when he was tense, and felt a flood of relief.

Because she wasn't imagining things.

He *did* feel it too.

Whatever *it* was.

Attraction.

Lust.

She doubted men like Julius suffered crushes.

Somehow, even if her five senses didn't really have anything to latch on to, she knew that he was working hard to contain whatever it was that kept him far over there with his whisky, rather than perched on her desk while they chatted.

It was actually a relief to know it was not just her.

Nice to glance up and see his jaw was clamped, to see him flash a polite smile. She knew it was mean—even as a little girl she had been mean sometimes... But, given that she was about to pass up a dream job, a new start, the first chance she'd ever had of a home and friends, she allowed herself a mean moment in the playground, rather than sitting scared at the water taps as she'd used to.

'I'll talk to him over the weekend,' she said.

'Of course.'

His voice had an edge—or was it a husk?—and she smiled to herself as she approved having a litter of Labrador puppies delivered to the stables for a photoshoot. The alternative was that she would cry, and she refused to do that.

'I'd better get going,' she said.

'Sure.'

She packed her bag, and finally the last zip had been

zipped and the last popper had been popped and she was on her way.

'Stay out of trouble,' Beatrice said, as she often did on leaving.

'Oh, believe me, I have been.'

She should have left then. She should have just nodded and wished him goodnight. But instead she fired a little dig as she hitched her bag onto her shoulder.

'To all intents and purposes...'

'Meaning?' His eyes narrowed.

'Nothing.'

She gave a wave as she left his office and headed down the corridor—not a dismissive wave, more a *leave it there* one. She closed her eyes as she walked, and wished she'd heeded her own advice. Because her little barb had only invited trouble—had only delayed the moment when she should have been halfway out of the building.

Julius wasn't leaving it there. 'Meaning?' he repeated.

Beatrice halted. Her eyes were still closed, and she took a deep breath and forced herself to be calm. She prayed her face wasn't as flushed as it felt as she opened her eyes and turned around.

'I've heard all about the secret passage to your residence.'

'Have you, now?'

'I'm just saying, given that your signing of the Document of Intent is imminent, now might be the time to be careful.'

'And there I was thinking you were here to tidy up my image, not police it.'

'You're right,' Beatrice conceded. 'I shouldn't have said anything.'

'Then why did you?'

* * *

He watched Beatrice as she looked skywards and took in a breath. She even opened her mouth to answer, but then closed it, clearly changing her mind.

And suddenly he saw the difference he had been unable to articulate earlier.

Those pale blue eyes were obscured, as if by two black saucers, and it wasn't just lust. She was angry—so angry he could see her attempts to contain it. He actually stood there, watching her trying to reel in all her unseen emotions. Like some teacher with a whistle, she was demanding they all get back in line, back in neat order.

But order could not be restored.

'I'm going to go,' Beatrice said. 'You've got an early flight.'

'Am I being told it's my bedtime now?'

'Julius, stop.'

'Stop what?' he checked insolently, as if he didn't know what the issue was…as if he couldn't feel the charge in the air between them that would not dim.

There was not a chance in hell of her being able to endure this every day for the rest of her working life, Beatrice knew. She was angry—but not with him. She was angry that she could not escape her own desire for him. She was angry at the circumstances that had brought her to this point.

And suddenly she could no longer hold it all in. She no longer wanted to.

'I don't really have a partner to discuss things with. I was trying to find a polite reason to turn the job offer down.'

'What's the real reason?'

'Believe me, you don't want to know.'

'Believe me, I do.'

Despite her inexperience, Beatrice instinctively knew that what she said next meant either goodnight or bed…

And Beatrice wanted it to be the latter.

She wanted to be the on-the-ball, confident, sexual woman he thought she was.

Just for one night.

Just to know.

Then she would be able to move on.

And she reminded herself in that dangerous moment of indecision that she'd once considered paying a stranger for that knowledge. One night with this reprobate prince meant she could get it for free. And not with a stranger.

Yes, she was angry. And suddenly all her carefully tamped-down emotions came boiling out of her in a rush.

'I'll tell you why I'll be turning your job offer down. I am so through with looking at pictures of you all day and reading about your sex life, watching the game you play of pretending to behave—'

'No one's pretending,'

She gave a disbelieving snort and immediately wished she hadn't. But it was out now, and so were her words. 'You've got your secret velvet love tunnel and you—'

'Beatrice!' He snapped her name.

She stopped and looked at him, and no one was pretending now. His black eyes were focussed on her mouth and then he moved those eyes up to hold hers. He took a strand of her hair and rubbed it between his fingers. Though his skin had not touched hers, and her hair had no sensation, the action was so intimate and so forbidden.

He put his glass down on the table beside her, and still she did not move. His hand cupped her cheek and they stared at each other.

'I've been told,' he said, 'by you, to be careful.'

'Yes.'

'No indiscretions. My liaison aide was most insistent…'

She should go. Absolutely, she should leave.

Beatrice knew she could remove his hand and tell him to keep on behaving; she knew she could leave if she wanted. Yet it felt as if the air in the room was shared: as he breathed in, so did she. She was rooted to the spot. Of course he must think she knew what she was doing. Possibly because right now Beatrice felt as if she did.

She already knew how to smile only for him, and she did that now…just a little. And she had touched his tie so many times when she closed her eyes and imagined him that it was almost rehearsed, and she played with the pointed end near his belt and felt the thick silk between her fingers.

'Perhaps she'd forgive one indiscretion.'

One.

He removed her bag from her shoulder and dropped it to the floor as if it displeased him.

A first kiss was supposed to be awkward, tentative, but she knew there was not a chance of him knowing that she was new to this, for there was no thinking, no anything, other than the relief of his lips brushing hers. Her head moved to one side to chase his mouth as he moved his lips to her cheek, to her eyes, then down to her neck, as though he were tasting her.

'Oh, God…' he said, as if he very much needed to.

And he moved his hands to hold her hips and kissed under her hair, burrowing at the side of her neck. His tongue was wet and his hands were steady. Beatrice arched her neck and he came up for air.

'Let's go through,' he suggested, with a hoarse edge to his voice, and then he lowered his lips again to hers and lingered there, until she parted to the slip of his whisky-laced tongue.

Beatrice sighed at this very new bliss, the slight shock of his tongue sliding against hers, the taste of her first kiss, and that sigh seemed to light something in them both. His mouth demanded more and more, his tongue parting her, tasting her deeper.

This was no typical first kiss; it was every kiss she had ever wanted. And she was kissing him back just as hard, knotting her hands in his newly cut hair and lost in bliss.

Her back was to the wall. His hands took hers from his head and held them against the wall so she was pinned there while he kissed her. He released her, but just for a second, so he could hitch her dress up and lift her so that she was able to wrap her legs around him.

Somehow he picked up her bag and started moving towards the door, and she realised he was taking her to bed. But even as they began to cross the room Beatrice began to slide down his body, and the moment she made contact with his buckle, and realised she was lodged against his erection, all those weeks of fighting it seemed pathetic—because nothing could have stopped this.

They couldn't even get to his apartment.

And now her bag was God knows where, and Jordan's desk was cleared in one swipe, and Beatrice's shoes were half off so she kicked them away.

Why, she asked herself, had she waited so long to know this, to allow this? To be on a desk with him parting her knickers as he kissed her ear, sucked her neck, and brought her closer to frantic completion than she'd imagined possible.

'Not here...'

It was Julius who was attempting to slow things down, even as she lifted her bottom to assist him in sliding her knickers off. He looked at her plain cotton multi-pack knickers and gave them no more consideration than Beatrice had when she'd purchased them. Rather he was looking at her pale blonde curls! And he'd clearly changed his mind about trying to get to the apartment. Instead he just slid her knickers down and got straight back to what he'd been doing.

'Or maybe here,' he said, parting her thighs.

He was no longer kissing her, and they were both watching him play with her shining pink lips, and as he stroked the little knot she'd long denied herself he groaned when she shivered beneath his touch.

Her throat was too constricted for her to speak, and she continued to watch him stroke her, fascinated not just at herself but at the sound of his response.

'Come on,' he said, as if she should be able to jump off the desk and walk steadily.

At the same time he was undoing his belt, and she watched as he so easily took himself out. Beatrice had never been more entranced, more scared and more thrilled, and somehow all at the same time. Her throat gave a little squeak that it had never emitted before.

He was so erect, almost indecent, that she shivered with new pleasure. Just the sight of his tip, stroking where his fingers had been, was enough to make her squeak again. She felt sick with pleasure as she touched the soft skin that belied the strength beneath. She ran a finger the length of a vein…all the way to the gleaming tip.

'Beatrice,' he warned. 'Bed *now*, or—'

'I know.'

But there was no stopping it as they both watched their flesh connect.

'Here,' Beatrice said.

Because she was scared that if her feet touched the

ground good sense would invade and she might never have this opportunity again.

And then even that became impossible, for at the first nudge of him she felt impaled. 'Julius…'

'I know…' He stopped. 'Have you got any…?'

She almost laughed at the fact that he thought she might have condoms in her work bag, in case she wanted to leap on a desk and have sex with someone.

Her head felt a little dizzy and she leant on him for a moment and could hear his heart thumping in his chest. 'No…'

'Then we—' He stopped, his erection batting against her inner thigh as he paused. 'Shh…' he warned, and looked not at her, but at the room that existed outside of them, listening to the sounds of the outside world and the shudder of the lift further down the corridor.

'No one must—' Beatrice was aghast.

He put a finger to her lips to hush her, and very deftly pulled her to her feet. Then he ran two hands down her hair to smooth it. 'Shoes!' he said.

She was shaking as she put them on, while he tucked himself away.

'Go and stand by the window,' he said.

She was too panicked to listen, and instead knelt down and scrambled to retrieve the contents of the desk, which had been tipped onto the floor.

'Leave it,' he warned, but at least he retrieved her knickers and passed them to her. 'Go to the window,' he said again.

Beatrice did. She stared down at the lake, holding her underwear like a bunched-up handkerchief in her hand. It was far too hard to reconcile her thoughts, so she just stared at the water and the silver birch and the white willow, and willed herself to appear as calm as the lake.

'*Signorina?*'

She turned her head and gave a brief smile to the guard. He nodded back, but then frowned at the spilled folders littering the floor.

Beatrice was trying to pluck a lie from the air to explain it, but then the guard saw Julius sitting there, apparently writing at the desk, and instead he gave Beatrice a small eye-roll and left.

She heard his footsteps disappear down the long passageway towards the Prince's residence. She looked down, half dreading that her dress would be at mid-thigh, or worse.

'You look fine,' Julius said. 'I mean, you look normal.'

Beatrice did not feel in the least normal.

She felt touched and kissed and still wanting.

But it felt so much better than wanting without having been touched or kissed.

'He'll be back in a few minutes,' Julius warned.

'How do I explain the folders?'

'You don't.' Julius shrugged and carried on pretending to write, or whatever it was he was doing at the desk on which he had nearly taken her just a few seconds ago.

He'd have found out that she was a virgin.

She breathed out slowly, to control her frantic heart.

And the palace doves, even with their clipped wings, would have taken flight when she screamed—because she was in no doubt, after that very brief glimpse, that it would have hurt.

Should she tell him?

How?

Just say, *Julius, I've never done this*? Or, *Julius, I'm actually a virgin.*

Beatrice could almost picture his wide eyes and the flash of awkwardness as he realised that the one-night stand he wanted came with a hymen and might require a little more—or a little *less*—than pure passion.

No.

Beatrice glanced over to the gleaming desk, where for the first time she'd felt unashamed and had wanted to know sheer pleasure. Just that.

Right now, she could not think further than that.

'Those shoes of his are killing me,' Julian groaned as the guard's shoes squeaked and clomped along the corridor towards them.

Squeak.

Clomp.

Squeak.

Clomp.

'If he goes out to the terrace for a smoke,' Julius whispered in a low voice, 'we'll make a run for it.'

'No!' Beatrice was on the edge of laughing, but changed it to a smile for the guard, who nodded as he walked past.

They heard every shudder of the ancient lift creaking its way up to collect him, but it was made bearable as Julius silently mouthed all that he intended to do to her as soon as they were alone.

She blushed, but nodded her assent.

'Thank God,' he said, when they were finally alone. But instead of carrying on where they'd left off he held her by the waist and looked down at her. 'I'm so glad that guard showed when he did.'

'Why?'

'I've been waiting for this.'

'So have I.'

It felt as if she'd been waiting all her life.

'Here,' he said, and took her jacket from the chair and passed it over to her, as well as her bag. 'We have a meeting to get to.'

She slipped on her jacket and flicked out her hair over the collar. 'One rule,' she said as they walked towards his residence. She felt so confident, so completely sure in this moment.

One night.

That was as safe as she could get.

No let-down.

No hurt.

No rejection.

Just this one night.

'One rule,' she said again as they reached the door to his apartment.

'I'm the same,' Julius agreed as he typed in a code. 'Don't worry. I've got plenty.'

He took her hand and led her inside. She had never even glimpsed inside his private residence. The ceilings were high and the floors were mosaic tiles, split by an emerald green carpet that ran the full length of the long corridor.

It looked to Beatrice as if it ran for a mile.

'I'm not talking about condoms,' she said.

'What, then?' he asked, not really waiting for an answer. 'Wait here,' he suggested. 'I'll just check someone's not turning back the bed or something...'

'You mean your staff could be in here?'

'There's a private lift,' he said. 'They could be preparing the bedroom suite.'

'Julius, I cannot be seen.'

'I am more than aware of that.' He was a little more specific. '*We* can't be seen.' He drew her into a lounge. 'So what's your one rule?'

So he had been listening.

'Just tonight.'

She saw the slightest frown pull his brows down.

'I mean it.' She did. 'No repeats. No hiding in corners

when you get back from your trip. We might get away with it once, but…'

She would not be his latest scandal. In fact, she would barely register as a blip; it was her own reputation she was guarding.

'Just tonight,' she said again.

'Don't make promises you can't keep.'

He gave her a smile that warned she might rue her words, but she was very familiar with arrogance. She knew that even though she might want desperately to know what it was like to make love to somebody, she would be able to walk away afterwards.

'Wait there,' he said. 'I'll go and check.'

She stood there in the lounge of the Prince's private apartment and tested her heart, grateful for the rule she'd spelt out.

One night was better than no nights. And, given her job, she had no 'reform-the-playboy' illusions.

None.

She looked at her surroundings and noted the plump leather sofas and chairs, the low music playing and the papers strewn across the table.

This was his home, for there was beautiful artwork on the walls, rather than stuffy old portraits, and there were collections of photos on occasional tables that told of happier times. Family times. It was odd to see the King smiling with his children, laughing with the Queen, looking like a father rather than a ruler. Still looking smart, but somewhat more casually dressed, with his errant son.

One photo was recent—well, a couple of years old maybe—and from the gorgeous temple and the blaze of orange trees Beatrice thought it looked like Japan. And there was a photo she almost recognised, similar to the one that had graced the covers of all the glossies when Julius had been born. Except it was a *before* photo.

Claude was lying on the bed, looking bored, Jasmine was clinging onto her mother, and the King was smiling down at his very large newborn baby. They were a family. It only really hit her then.

She picked up a photo of the three siblings. She guessed Julius to be fifteen, maybe sixteen, in it. Claude's face looked so serious compared to Julius's smile, and then she looked at Jasmine. Her smile was so wide it took a second for her to see there was tape on her face and a tube that ran into her nose. Beatrice looked at the protruding collarbones and pale, veiny hands and saw that Jasmine had clearly been very ill.

Was she the little grey cygnet?

Had that been what Julius had been trying to tell her as they'd sat by the lake…?

Was this to do with the promise that had been made?

Guilt washed over her as it dawned on her that it might not be ego that was keeping him from changing the line of succession but love for his sister…a desire to protect her. He had to keep his promise and protect his fragile sister.

But why couldn't they just give him a moment to breathe, instead of bombarding him with constant demands to step into his brother's shoes and take a wife?

Beatrice jumped as the door opened and Julius returned. She turned to look at him, but now she saw him through different eyes and it was impossible to go back to before she knew.

'Hey…' he said, bathing her with his smile. 'We won't be disturbed.'

He offered her his hand, and suddenly she desperately needed it, because the emerald carpet felt like a glass bridge beneath her feet…or a suspension bridge across a vast ravine. She was clinging onto his hand, both nervous and excited at the danger of adventure and secrets...

His bedroom suite, his most private abode, was decorated in dark, inky silk, from the walls to the drapes, while the thick carpet was the colour of mist rising. French windows led to a terrace, but she barely glimpsed it, for he clicked a button and the drapes fell and plunged them briefly into darkness. Then soft lights came on, and it felt like a late summer's night with the air still holding the heat.

'Take your jacket off,' Julius said, and as she did so Beatrice found that the slight frown his request had evoked in her faded into a smile as she realised that she had not been imagining any of this.

This?

This interest.

For now, in his suite, he could watch as she hung her jacket over a chair even as he'd tried not to watch her before.

It was different now, though.

Different because his eyes roamed her body, and she liked their perusal as she delicately draped her jacket on his bedroom chair.

Different because Beatrice did not have to flick her eyes away, or deny that she was burning too.

Different because they were both smiling at each other.

She'd expected to feel shy, yet with only desire facing her Julius made it impossible for her to feel that way—as if her shyness had been erased, as if it had never existed.

'Shoes,' he said, and she slipped off her ballet flats.

She stood a quarter of an inch smaller, yet she walked tall as she went over to him.

'Your tie annoys me,' Beatrice said, and took in her hand the half-undone silk. 'It should be on or off.'

'Take it off, then.'

Whatever she wanted to do, she could, and so she took off his tie, and then undid the buttons of his shirt, looked at the fan of dark hair and the dark flat nipples. She ran her arms across his broad shoulders and down his long arms, then stretched up to kiss him. She tasted him, and explored how it felt to linger there.

He removed his shirt as they kissed, and almost growled in impatient desire as he unzipped her dress, for they were both aching for the touch of each other's skin.

No one had seen her less than completely dressed since she was a child, but he made it so nice, stroking the sides of her ribs as if they were made entirely for the purpose of being stroked like that.

'Lift your arms,' he said as he unhooked her bra, and she acquiesced to his odd request, and then shivered as he stroked those ribs until she had no choice but to rest her arms on his shoulders. Then he cupped her small breasts with his warm palms and she felt the pleasure of his interest, not just the tease of his touch.

He moved down to her hips and then cupped her bottom. He pressed his fingers into the flesh, but gently, as if testing the ripeness of a piece of fruit. He spun her quickly, she didn't quite know how, so he could feast his eyes on her bottom, and then he brought her back to face him…

His erection was pressed against her stomach, and he cupped her bottom again and rocked her against him. And of all the surprises that this experience was bringing—and for Julius there were many—this one felt the most intimate. For when he'd thought about Beatrice—and of course he had imagined what her naked body would look like—he had thought she might be a little bony. Yet in the flesh she was softer than his experienced eye had considered.

Julius felt as if he'd been let in on a secret—as if he was

the only one who knew that beneath her grey, shapeless shift dresses her bottom was plump and her breasts were pert. She was soft and inviting, rather than the guarded, prickly woman she seemed to be outside of his bedroom.

Now she was kissing his chest and tasting his flat nipples, before going up onto tiptoe, and the motion was as beautiful and as rare as a thorny cactus flowering in the desert.

For they, too, flowered for just one night.

'I like this,' Beatrice said.

She was tasting his salty skin and feeling his hands roaming across her bottom, but he peeled her off him.

'Lie down,' he told her, and picked her up and made her do so himself.

His bed was as big as her whole basement office, and she felt swallowed whole by dark velvet. She lifted herself up to her elbows, so she could drink in his lean body, and the flat stomach and hips that seemed too narrow for what stood erect between them.

He was muscled, yet in subtle long lines, and as he turned away to go to his dresser she saw his taut buttocks and the power of his back, all the restrained energy he held within.

'I love your scent,' he told her, as he rolled a condom down his length and she tried to fathom that within her.

'I don't wear any.'

'You have horrible soap…'

'Ouch.' She winced.

'But then it fades and I get your scent…'

'Oh.'

'Doctor's soap,' he said as he prowled towards her on the bed and knelt over her.

She felt his eyes scan the path to treasure. First, though, he bent and kissed her shoulder.

'It's gone now.'

He lightly kissed the same breast he had so gently teased with his fingers, and then he bent and took her nipple deep into his mouth. She failed in an attempt to sit up and just lay there, swallowing at the shock of pleasure his actions had provoked.

He sucked harder, and then released her, and then sucked harder again. He took her hand and placed it on the breast he'd ignored, as if he expected her to caress herself, but when she just lay there he pinched her nipple for her and played with both willingly.

'Yes,' she said, and he kissed lower and lower, down her taut stomach which was held tight in anticipation.

'Relax,' he told her, his hand between her legs.

She'd thought she was relaxed, and told him so.

'Beatrice…' He knelt up and parted her legs, and still she was not shy.

Beatrice had never thought that she might lie there and feel hot breath on her sex as a handsome prince stroked her curls, that she might laugh as he told her that *here* she tasted of doctor's soap.

But then there was no breath left for laughing, because he'd buried his tongue inside her, his fingers caressing her thighs, so that somehow his mouth soothed her sex.

Beatrice held his head at first, but then gave in and raised her arms instead, grasping air, wishing for a bed-head or something to hold on to.

She wanted to arch her back, but he held her hips down. There was a mute protest within her, a refusal to succumb to the pressure of his mouth, and yet she was writhing beneath him.

'Julius…' she panted.

She didn't know what to do with herself. Initially she'd wanted to push him away—but she'd resisted doing so, for she liked the demand of his intimate kiss, liked the intensity of it. And as she lay there it was if she was falling backwards, as if the bed beneath them no longer supported her, and she was falling back just to experience the sensation over and over again. The flood of pleasure doused the sting of shame at her own guilty allowance of it.

He moaned, and he tasted her, and she did not know how to enjoy it. She just knew that she did—far too much.

'Julius...' His hands were at the very tops of her thighs, his tongue insistent, and finally she gave in to the pressure that was building inside her.

But it seemed it was not enough for Julius. He held her hips and tasted deeper, silently demanded more, but she pulled back.

'I want you now,' Beatrice said, her voice hoarse yet her demand clear.

He looked up to her and seemed surprised that even as she was on the edge of climax she still held her control.

And now, as he levered himself up and over her, she attempted to control his actions even more.

'Slowly,' she said.

'Don't bother,' he said, and they both knew he did not play by the rules, and she would not be dictating their pace, or denying their heat, or expecting to fool him that she had let go completely.

Beatrice should perhaps have rued her own naivety then, or considered this a reckless mistake, but it was overridden by the certainty that she had chosen well.

There was no one else she could be naked with, as close to trusting as she dared to be, and every nerve, every pore, said, yes, this had to be.

His face was wet from her sex and his kiss tasted a little of her. She gave a soft laugh into his mouth because, yes, beneath the antiseptic soap there was musk and citrus to explore.

It was a deliciously slow kiss. And her head really was falling back this time, for he'd dashed the pillows off the bed so she lay flat beneath him, hungry for more. His hand stroked a burning path down her body and parted her legs, and then he guided himself to where she ached.

'I want you so much,' she admitted.

'I want you too,' he affirmed.

He was ready to glide into her, to sink into bliss, but was met with unexpected resistance. Not protest—no, there was no protest. But he pulled back a fraction, heard her pant, and the slight cry at his second attempt to enter her.

She was reaching up to kiss him, trying to distract him, as if he should politely not notice the virgin in his bed.

He pulled his head back and realised he *was* the only one who knew the softness and flesh beneath her plain grey shift dresses. The only one to witness this rare flower bloom.

He met her eyes and smiled a secret smile as she gave the smallest nod. 'Please…' she breathed.

Julius obliged, and seared in.

Her sob as he tore her flesh came from deep within, and yet she supressed it, holding it in her taut throat as he watched intently.

Julius gave her a slight pause as she tried to acclimatise to his slow strokes, like a breathless walker insisting that she was okay, that she could keep up, certain they were almost there.

His scrutiny was obviously too much, and as he began to move rhythmically she covered her eyes with her arm, trying to breathe through the pain. She wanted to hide, but he removed her arm from her face and refused to allow it.

Too late to hide, his eyes told her, though he did not say it out loud.

Beatrice found out that his first few thrusts had been but a gentle introduction, because this time when he pulled back, when she thought she knew what it would be like, he drove in and gave her every inch of him, and she thought she might split in two.

She let out a desperate shout.

He swore, but very quietly and rather nicely.

He wasn't being still to be nice. In fact, he told her, he was fighting not to come.

They stared at each other in incredible silence, as if trying not to disturb something. And when he resumed his rhythm, so too did the pain resume, and her moan could not be supressed—not that she tried.

As it faded he repeated his movement slowly, repeated and repeated. At first the cocktail of pain and pleasure was too heady a mix for Beatrice to make sense of, but the first bolts of pain were receding, spinning away to become pleasure as Julius's deepest strokes chased away the hurt.

He took one leg and angled it, positioning her and opening her more. It felt so good that she did the same with the other leg, so that both her knees were up. He closed his eyes and pushed in and drew out slowly, breathing hard as his features sharpened.

She wanted to watch him so badly, but Beatrice closed her own eyes—not to hide, but to lose herself in the moment, entirely overwhelmed by sensation.

'Don't stop...' she panted, because she was coming

more undone with every stroke, every stretch within her, and every breath of his was a measured exhalation beckoning her on.

Her hands moved to his buttocks and up to his muscled back, and then her hips moved, as if they had decided to go it alone, for she'd given no conscious instruction for them to do so.

'Oh, God...'

She wished time would stop, so she could catch her breath, ease the taut pull of her thighs and the building pressure inside her, but then she realised how tame her cry had been. For he was the one who was suppressing his cries now, and there was no longer any measured exhalation, no slow, relentless rhythm.

It was his turn to lose control.

He braced himself high up on his forearms and began to move faster. Beatrice watched with pleasure as he pounded out a rhythm that felt as if it was building to something still out of reach. She noted how his eyes closed as he took her harder, how his rapid sounds did not equate to the intimacy of the caress taking place deep within her.

'Julius...' she whispered, and then she lifted her hips to him, felt a kind of white heat zap her spine, and gave in to the urge to turn in his arms, to escape what he'd unleashed—a pleasure far too deep.

And yet he dragged it from her, demanded it of her, so that she was panting and spent and yet still somehow restrained. She had resisted letting go all the way even as she'd pulsed around him. Even as she'd arched into him she'd pulled back.

'No, no,' he told her. 'No more hiding.'

Beatrice knew she was crying, but this time they were not lonely, hopeless tears. This time they were frantic ones.

She had played with fire and now she was burning, for it was a pleasure that felt too acute, too much, too good to be real.

'*Vengo*...' she told him in Italian. She was coming. Almost.

They were locked in battle—him desperate to release, Beatrice on the edge and refusing to leap—but then he thrust one final powerful time and she tensed with that last push.

He shouted an airless cry that marshalled the white heat back to the very base of her spine, tapping fresh reserves as he shot into her and made her a liar—for *now* she shattered.

The intensity startled Beatrice, who was almost cross that he could summon these pulses and this energy... could coil her so tight and then hit release whenever he wanted.

At last, tension released, he stroked her stomach as if coaxing out the last from himself and from her, and then he slid out of her and collapsed on top of her. They lay in silence until the need to breathe overtook them both and he rolled off.

Beatrice knew he was looking at her, but she kept her eyes closed, gulping in air. Only now was she a little scared—she had no idea what to do, what was supposed to happen next.

Dizzy and sated, Julius lay on his side, one arm supporting his head, and watched her flickering eyelashes. It was as if she was pretending to be asleep, and it somehow made him smile.

'Beatrice...?' Usually he spoke so easily, so comfortably about sex, yet he knew she was hiding now, here in his bed, and did not quite know how to address that. 'Are you okay?'

'Very,' she said without opening her eyes.

And that was the only thing she really knew.

Just that she felt very, very okay…

CHAPTER EIGHT

JULIUS WAS VERY nice to sleep with.

As in *sleep* with.

Of all the events today, the one that surprised Beatrice the most was that instead of asking difficult questions he'd pulled her in and she'd fallen completely to sleep—and she would have remained there had it not been for the buzz of her work phone.

'Why didn't you turn it off?' he said, as her eyes opened to the intrusion.

'What time is it?' She frowned.

'Maybe ten?'

As she went to sit up and retrieve her phone he shook his head.

'Leave it,' he told her.

'It might be important.'

'This is important.'

Julius had not been asleep. He was up on one arm and his hand was warm on her stomach, drawing light circles and looking down at where his fingers traced shapes on her skin. He looked as if he was considering—quite what she didn't know.

Julius was, in fact, trying to heed his own advice and not go for the jugular. Not ask *What the hell?*

He did *not* sleep with virgins.

With one possible exception: his future bride.

He'd actually been crossing his fingers that his bride wouldn't be a virgin! If he was honest, he wasn't really looking forward to it—any of it. The wedding, the wedding night, the forced conversation, a month stuck on an island with a stranger...

That, though, was a side issue.

Such a side issue that he shoved the thought away and looked at the pale skin beneath his fingers, at the red tips of the blonde curls, visible evidence of her former virginity.

Julius did not sleep with virgins because he liked very uncomplicated sex—preferably with a lover who accepted that he could only partake in a casual relationship...one who shared the pleasure, smiled, dressed and left.

But he didn't want Beatrice to do that yet, even though she was already moving to sit up.

'I ought to go...'

'Hey...' he found himself saying. 'We should at least be able to talk.'

'About what?' she asked. 'Julius, there are so many parts of you I'm not allowed to know.'

'For good reason.'

'Well, I have my own reasons,' she said.

'If I'd known—'

'If you'd known then you'd have never...' Beatrice said. 'Do you know why?'

'Because you'd have been worried I'd get all clingy, demand more...'

He could almost feel the prickles rising on the skin that had only just now been so smooth beneath his fingers. He didn't stop her—not because he agreed, but because he wanted her to continue.

* * *

'You'd have worried that I'd want presents and phone calls, instead of just sex with someone gorgeous to whom I'm attracted.'

Beatrice paused, and those circles he was drawing on her stomach were like a beckoning...a soft caress so inviting she wanted to admit that while she was telling the truth she was perhaps possibly lying a little too.

It had nothing to do with her virginity, though. Beatrice knew she could have slept with a hundred men prior to this and she would still want more of him.

But then she swallowed, because he was the only man she'd felt able to sleep with. Not just sleep with...lie with, talk to, flirt with, smile at...

Was it more than a crush?

Or were all these lovely endorphins and the lull of his hand smudging her senses and letting her think it could be more...?

'Well, you don't have to worry,' she told him. 'I was actually going to hire someone...'

'Were you, now?'

His finger did not stop moving.

'Just to get it over and done with.'

'Over and done with?' He smiled a little at her choice of words, and it was a smile she could not read.

'I was going to have him take me out for my thirtieth and get me Birthday Girl Martinis and...'

'What is your obsession with this drink?'

'I've never had one,' she admitted. 'I heard Jordan talking about them the other week.'

'What else was your for-hire man going to do?' he asked.

She wanted his eyes to reveal anger or jealousy, but instead they were warm with curiosity.

'I hadn't decided.'

'Why not for your twenty-ninth?'

'I only just decided.'

'To get it over and done with?'

'Yes.'

'Do you know, a century ago—?'

'Don't worry. I was never expecting marriage.'

'Well, you'd never have got it. Unless you have a couple of countries tucked away that you haven't told me about. Even then it would have to go to counsel—'

'Never expecting to be your mistress, then.' She glared. 'Your hetaera, or whatever you call them.'

'Oh, no.' He shook his head. 'You'd need serious connections to get that title.'

It hurt, but she knew he wasn't wrong.

'I don't make the rules, Beatrice. I live them. A century ago you would have had your choice of gold amulet.'

Beatrice met his eyes and even laughed. 'Well, luckily it's not a century ago—and anyway, I told you I'm allergic to gold.'

'Nobody's allergic to gold.'

'Well, I am. It brings me out in welts.' She pushed away his hand. 'I'm going to have a shower.'

'No, no…' he said. 'I haven't yet told you why I don't sleep with virgins.'

'Go ahead!'

'Because, as you know, I don't get to have close friends. Nor do I get to have relationships.'

'Come off it!' She blew a sharp breath out from her mouth. After all, she had spent the last few months dealing with the fallout of his relationships…

'Listen to me,' he warned, in a voice that told her he was completely serious. 'I don't get to be close to anyone unless it's family, or my future bride.'

'What? Now that you're the heir?'

'No.' He shook his head. 'Always. I told you. I wasn't even allowed close friends.'

Yes, he had told her that.

'I have had relationships—but not deep ones. Not a single one. I have always known that my wife will be chosen with politics in mind, and with an understanding that should the unthinkable happen she would be queen consort.'

'What has that to do with me?'

'Nothing,' he told her. 'At all.'

She swallowed.

'And that is why I ensure my partners are always very content to keep things light.'

'Well, lucky for you this virgin is.'

She climbed out of bed and he glanced down at her thighs. There was no need to point out she was a virgin no more.

'I'll have a body shower,' she told him.

'A *body* shower?'

She was not going to stand there and explain it to him. 'And then I'll get dressed and go out there and look like I'm working.'

'Beatrice, you are not going back to your desk and then getting the shuttle bus home.'

'What? Will you call your driver to take me home? I *know* him, Julius. If you could just check the corridor and make sure the guard's not doing his rounds again?'

'Are you regretting this already?'

'No.'

'I don't believe you.'

'I honestly am not,' Beatrice said. 'Though I might if we're found out.'

She made a pertinent point.

'I'm not worrying about your reputation, Julius. I know I wouldn't merit a blip even if this got out. I'm looking after my own. I get it, okay?'

Oh, no, you don't.

He lay back as she flounced off to the bathroom. He wanted to redo that conversation. But then again, best not.

It wasn't only Beatrice getting involved that concerned him.

Just sex, he'd thought, and then she would be out of his head.

Well, it had sounded like a plan.

Damn!

The bathroom was bathed in instant golden light. Midas must have touched everything in here, Beatrice thought, staring at the golden walls.

Oh, God. She'd told him her gigolo plan.

She'd been trying to convince him of how little this mattered to her, and yet somehow he'd rather deftly coaxed out that this plan had only occurred to her in recent weeks.

She would have loved to step under the full blast of the shower and pelt away her thoughts, but wet hair might be a giveaway, so she took the handheld part and rinsed her body, and tried to deny how much she liked him.

Really, *really* liked him.

Oh, God. She was in way over her head and lying through her clenched teeth.

But it didn't matter—she wasn't even mistress material! Not that she wanted to be one.

She dressed, and was surprised by the normality of her own reflection. It revealed nothing of the burn between her legs, or the ache of her breasts, and so, reassured by that, she stepped out.

'Body shower,' he said when he saw her dry hair. 'I get it now.'

She managed a smile.

'Do you want a drink, or some dinner?'

'I've had some water.'

'I can do better than the bathroom tap.'

'I know,' Beatrice said. 'But I do think it's better if I just go.'

'If that's what you want.'

'It is. Can you check the exit?'

'Sure.'

'If anyone asks I'll just say I was kept late making drafts.'

'Then they'll know you're lying,' Julius said. 'Since when do you make excuses for working late?'

True...

Walking back down the emerald carpet, she felt so different. She'd been so sure, so confident that she could handle this, and yet she felt an overwhelming temptation to turn, to go back to his bed, to be with him all over again.

'I'll see you in a week,' he said, trying to test this new normal between them.

'Yes.'

She nodded and reached for the door, and it dawned on him then that Beatrice might take this week to conjure up a family emergency, or some such.

And that would be it.

'Beatrice?' he halted her. 'I'll see you in a week?'

Beatrice heard what was beneath his question this time. He was asking if she was lying about being able to handle this. If she really had just wanted to lose her virginity on a Friday after work.

Well, as far as he was concerned she had.

The rest he didn't get to see.

Aside from that, it would be Jordan writing her reference. Not him!

'Of course,' she said. And then she had to execute the bravest part of the night as she turned and gave his taut mouth a kiss. 'It was a lovely night.'

The office was exactly as they'd left it. She should pick up the folders, really, return order to the place. But instead Beatrice just headed for the exit and took the stairs down.

The night smelt like rain, except the sky was clear. Very deliberately, she didn't look up or back, just gulped in air—and then stilled when she saw a figure by the lake.

The King.

Guilt made her jump, but palace staff knew how to be discreet and make themselves invisible, and so she took the long way round, through the rose garden, and tried to pretend she hadn't seen what she had.

'*Signorina...*' the shuttle bus driver said as he nodded in greeting.

No Cinderella's carriage turning back into a pumpkin for her, she thought darkly—just the shuttle bus home.

As the bus took her along Prince's Lane she sat with her head against the window, nodding when they stopped at the porter's lodge and a few familiar faces climbed on.

The best part was when the guards got on at the main gates for a random bag check, in case she'd pinched a pepper pot or something.

And then she felt teary.

And not just for herself but for Julius too.

Loneliness came in so many forms.

Then she thought of the King, staring into the lake and wiping his eyes, and that had her wondering if her allergies were starting again.

Kings weren't supposed to cry.

CHAPTER NINE

'Sir?'

Julius opened his eyes, which he had closed not to sleep but in order to take a couple of moments to assimilate his thoughts—or had he actually dozed off?

He glanced out of the plane window. But even orientated to the real world now, as the plane sliced through the dawn, Julius felt as if he was hurtling in the wrong direction.

'Sir?' It was the flight attendant again.

'No.' He declined the offer of breakfast. 'No, thank you.'

They were over the edge of the archipelago, where the ocean met the red sky as if the seabed was littered with fiery opals. There was Regalsi, the remotest island, with its unique red sands, far in the distance.

Looking out, Julius refused to think of his honeymoon. *Hell.* He was signing the Document of Intent soon; he'd been putting it off until *she* was gone...

Now he didn't want her to go at all.

He'd been resigned to marriage, ready to assume his duty, until she'd arrived to shine up his image.

'Do you want to go through this now?' Jordan broke into his thoughts. 'Or sleep first?'

'No, let's get it done.'

It was mainly practical—just last-minute changes to the

itinerary and a speech, a poem he was supposed to read in Pontic Greek for his brother…

'You've practised?' Jordan asked.

He rolled his eyes.

'I figured it wasn't going so well when I saw you'd swiped all the things off my desk, so I found a recording of it for you to listen to…'

And the worrying part—the seriously worrying part— was that Julius wanted to reach for his phone and share a little private smile with Beatrice.

He didn't share private smiles with anyone.

Ever.

'Can you cast your eyes over this?' Jordan handed him a file.

'What is it?' Julius frowned even as he read it.

'A list of possibilities for a permanent liaison aide,' Jordan said, and then added, 'I like the second one; he's got two royal weddings under his belt.'

He nodded, and had to carry on as if he cared not at all that Beatrice had clearly declined the job offer.

It was odd to be mid-air and to register that he really did care. Far too much.

Not that she'd declined the permanent role—he'd already known that she would—what he cared about was whether she had declined it before or after going to bed with him.

Had she fired off a text just after she'd left his bed?

Was she coming back?

'Jordan?' he checked, seemingly oh-so-casually. 'I thought you were going to speak with Beatrice about a permanent role?'

'I did, but she wasn't interested.'

'So she formally turned it down?'

'Beatrice took herself out of the running. I spoke to

her straight after you did.' Jordan was head-down and writing in margins. 'But, no. She prefers short-term contracts, she said.'

Julius was looking at last night through different eyes now, realising Beatrice had known all along that she was leaving. The whole 'I have to talk to my partner' thing had been purely to provoke a reaction from him.

Well, she certainly had.

He should feel played, and yet he did not.

Used? No.

He just sat there trying to make sense of last night, and frowned in irritation when Jordan spoke on, interrupting his thoughts.

'I don't think that's all there was to it, though,' Jordan said, but offered no more.

It was hard not to prompt his PA, because he wouldn't usually take such a deep interest in a temp, but when Jordan went back to her writing it was clear that if he wanted to know more then he had no choice but to ask.

'What, then?'

'I don't think she wanted the hassle of the enhanced security check.'

Julius had *not* been expecting that. 'What?'

'Her initial clearance flagged a name-change at nineteen.' Jordan glanced up, perhaps thinking she was being scrutinised. 'But Beatrice was fully cleared for basic access, sir. There's been no breach…'

'Of course not.' He shook his head. 'What does her name-change have to do with things?'

'She was schooled in Trebordi.' Jordan gave him a look that he presumed was supposed to say it all.

'Sicily?' he said.

'She was raised in the convent at Trebordi—it's like Di Dio Bellanisiá,' she said, citing their national equivalent.

Julius felt his blood run cold.

Di Dio Bellanisiá was a convent infamous for its baby wheel, though it was maintained there now only for sentimental purposes and history, not for its original purpose. He had visited it, even spoken with some families who had a parent or grandparent who had been raised there.

Still, on occasion a baby was left there… Abandoned.

'I don't think she wanted anyone raking through her past. I can't say I blame her.' Jordan suddenly winced. 'Oh!'

'Jordan?'

'It's nothing, sir.'

'Don't do that,' he warned. 'There's nothing more irritating than someone saying, *Oh, it's nothing…*'

They'd had this conversation before, so it wasn't anything new. Usually it was caused by Julius's irritation at something Jordan had said, followed by boredom when she actually told him about the *nothing* that had suddenly occurred to her…

This wasn't nothing, though.

'I've been pushing her to come to the Flower Festival,' Jordan said. 'That was when I knew I'd be offering her a permanent role. I thought she was being rude when she said she doesn't like festivals.'

'I don't much like them, either,' he said.

'Her surname used to be Festa.'

He knew enough from his visits to Di Dio Bellanisiá and other places like it that there wasn't great thought given to the surnames of the children left there.

Festa. Festival.

What the word meant to her, he didn't know, but clearly it meant enough that she had changed her name.

'Was she okay about it?' He wasn't completely thoughtless; if it was anyone else he'd have asked too. At least he hoped he would...

'She seemed to be. Who really knows with Beatrice?'

Not he. He thought of her snapping whenever he'd broached her past, or her English surname, and then he recalled her red swollen eyes after her birthday weekend.

He realised he'd completely misread the situation— for she really had given him a piece of herself when she'd shared something about her long-lost friend. Her so-called twin, yet not a blood relation, and how she'd gone back to find her and then decided things were better left...

Julius had no choice but to leave things.

It didn't make him feel better, though.

Where Beatrice was concerned, it didn't feel best left. Even if he knew it would be far more sensible to do so.

CHAPTER TEN

BEATRICE CHECKED HER heart several times throughout the weekend, like a nurse taking a pulse at intervals, but it was beating steadily.

She dealt with casual sex and its fallout for a living, and she certainly wasn't going to fall apart herself.

She was very grateful to have a week's reprieve before facing him, though.

Work was quiet. As well as Julius being away, the King was visiting the other islands all week, and it felt like that time between Christmas and New Year, when there was only a skeleton staff and nothing really happened.

It was just quiet.

Incredibly so.

Sometimes painfully so.

While the cats were away, the mice hit the snooze button…

And then suddenly he called.

That day even the lazy peacocks were up by the time Beatrice had disembarked the shuttle bus and was walking along Prince's Lane. Then her phone rang, and she heard his voice for the first time since that night.

'Are you in my offices or downstairs?'

'Downstairs,' Beatrice lied, and stared at the peacock, daring it to screech.

'No problem. I'll find someone else.'

He rang off, and there was a tiny little spike on her temperature chart—a little flash of indignation that he hadn't so much as said hello or asked if she was okay.

It was solved by a couple of deep breaths, and then a nervous lick of her lips. Because she'd been walking with her phone in her hand when usually it lived in her bag until she arrived at work. Always.

Do not go there, Beatrice warned herself, and threw her phone into her bag.

Yet, it was true.

Be very careful what you wish for, she thought.

Beatrice might have demanded discretion, but Julius was taking it to a whole new level.

There was nothing—not a hint, not a breath of change in his texts, and nor, when he called again, in his tone.

'Please ensure there is no mention in the media of my trip to my mother's home.'

'Of course.'

'No confirmation I was there.'

'Sir.' She took a breath and then addressed the latest PR issue—though they were becoming comparatively few. 'There's a rather tasteless article regarding the Marchioness.'

'Okay.'

He rang off, and she breathed out, and insisted again to herself that nothing had changed.

It had *always* irked her, the way he just called and didn't introduce himself, nor said hi or bye.

Then, late on Friday, speaking with Jordan just before the entourage prepared to head home, Beatrice found out that the Marchioness had been sent flowers, and that Jordan had spoken at length with her to mollify her regarding the article in the press.

'She can be temperamental,' Jordan explained, and rang off.

You are not temperamental, Beatrice reminded herself, over and over.

You are not temperamental, she told herself, when for the first time she had to cancel her Saturday Mandarin lesson because she hadn't done her prep.

Which meant she'd have two weeks to catch up on.

And her laundry wasn't done, she realised as she pulled on her last pair of clean knickers.

All her routines had gone to pot.

She threw her washing into the machine and filled the dishwasher, happy to have things restored to their usual order.

Except she was doing housework in her knickers.

Selecting a lemon cheesecloth dress better suited to a day at the beach than a walk along the smart marina, she was determined to face the day.

She tied on espadrilles, put on a big hat and sunglasses, and put her headphones in, deciding it was easier to focus on Mandarin rather than the fact that Julius was due back this morning. Even if Mandarin was the hardest language to master for a Latin-loving girl.

The marina was practically deserted.

Even her favourite coffee shop was closed.

It was like a dystopian world, Beatrice thought as she took out her headphones. There was barely a soul around. And then suddenly there were cannons firing. They very often did here, only it seemed more than usual today— and then it dawned on her that she was possibly the only person in the country not at the Flower Festival.

Despite her aversion to all things *festa*, Beatrice found herself arriving there. It was nothing like the festival at

Trebordi. There it was all bright lights and carnival music, but here it was flowers, and more flowers, and food.

It was relaxed too. She saw Jasmine's daughter Arabella with her best friend, and security guards following very discreetly behind them.

If she'd been staying, Beatrice would have bought some tulip bulbs to put in a pot on her balcony. Instead she bought some local beeswax lip balm from one of the little stalls, an insulating cup that promised six hours of heat for her coffee, and then decided to see if she could find some sunscreen as the sun was beating on her exposed shoulders.

During her search, she happened upon one of the Greek stalls and stood inhaling *sapoúni*. Soap. It smelt…not quite like him, but there was a beautiful bergamot note, and there was another with a jasmine scent …

Princess Jasmine! Beatrice wandered towards the stage, curious to hear Jasmine's speech, as were the women behind her.

'*Bella, bella…*'

They were chatting about her lovely family, and how soft-spoken she was, and then about the late Prince Claude. Beatrice really wished she'd done some of this listening before now, because their conversation had turned to Julius.

'Dear, dear, dear…'

One of them tutted, and then the other, but they started to laugh, and as it turned out they loved Julius.

So too did the people ahead of her, whose conversation she listened to next.

She heard more gossip in those few moments than she could ever have found in newspaper articles, and more affection for Julius than the palace had ever admitted.

People commented on his bachelor status, but without the frantic air of his family and aides, and she wished she could somehow convey to them that the word on the street seemed to be that he should take his time.

But if she did then it would sound as if she had an agenda. And maybe she did. Because she kept having little visions of them somehow managing to see each other, even for a short while. And then the bubble was dispersing, and she realised how distracted he made her—because she still hadn't put on sunscreen and her shoulders were starting to redden.

'What time is Princess Jasmine speaking?' she asked the woman beside her.

'No,' she was informed. 'Prince Julius.'

Beatrice wanted to correct her, because she'd just seen Arabella with her nanny, and she knew the palace schedule after all, but she just nodded and smiled and made her way to the gathered crowd.

She heard cheers drown out the music as, yes, Julius came onto the stage.

He looked fantastic and dreadful all in one. He was dressed in full military uniform, and that too was unexpected. The grey and Prussian blue check and the black boots were too much for the heat, but he was so handsome. He looked fresh and crisp, and yet she could see there was a pallor to his features, and those cheekbones were even more prominent.

'We had to ask the pilot to catch a tail wind so I could be here…' he told his delighted audience. But he was thrilled to have made it.

Oh, and the people were thrilled to see him.

As was she.

It was hard to reconcile the fact that the last time she had, they'd just been in bed together.

For a whole week she'd somehow handled his business

texts and complete lack of anything else because he hadn't been there, but now he was.

And it stung.

Even more than the sun beating on her shoulders.

Come on, Beatrice, she told herself, *you played with the playboy. You invited the hurt. It was you who wanted adventure...wanted to get it over and done with...*

How she wished Alicia was still in her life, because she wanted someone to explain to her why she was waiting breathlessly for his eyes to land on hers. Wishing he might suddenly notice her in the crowd. Might give her a smile or react in some way.

But he just kept on with his off-the-cuff speech...talking about the flowers. How from the plane he had seen every island, ablaze with colour...

'The same colours that greeted our soldiers when they returned from war.'

He spoke of the past, of how the islanders had almost lived underground in bunkers and how root vegetables had been their sustenance, and of the island's vital part in the World Wars.

He said how good it was to have their beloved Flower Festival back after its absence last year. 'I know the King has visited all the islands this week, and he insists he does not have a favourite...' He gave them a dubious look...

Julius was flirting with them.

Charmingly.

Easily.

And in such a way that all were convinced that this island was his favourite.

How easily he won them over with his teasing.

Then he spoke of Prince Claude, and the devastating flu that had ravaged the islands. And then he returned to speak of the flowers again, and how they brought a smile to people's faces and brightened the most difficult of days…

Perhaps for the Marchioness, Beatrice thought bitterly, watching as he left the stage and the crowd started to disperse.

Oh, she did not want to be feeling like this. It was supposed to be a crush, or just sex—not this lurch in her chest at the sight of him. Not those bats all flying out of their caves and swooping at the sound of his deep voice.

She was so awkward, so emotionally inept, that she'd probably have fallen for her gigolo, Beatrice tried to insist to herself. It was infatuation, lust—whatever label she could put on it.

Because it could not be anything more than that.

It just could not be.

'Beatrice!'

She turned at the sound of her name.

It was Jordan, with a suited man whom Beatrice took to be Stavros, but there was no introduction.

'Have you seen Despina?' Jordan asked.

'No.'

Poor Jordan must be exhausted, given they had only landed that morning. Her hair was all frizzed from a week of humidity, and she had an air of grim determination on her face.

'We're going over to the marquee,' Jordan said, and then frowned at Beatrice's bare shoulders. 'Beatrice, I told you about the dress code. And where's your lanyard?'

'I'm not here for the marquee.'

She so wasn't—though admittedly her shoulders were on fire and she thought some shade would be nice. But she knew she was beyond underdressed.

'I wasn't planning to come. How come Princess Jasmine didn't—?'

'It was always the plan to have the Prince, a soldier who has served in the military, make the speech. Princess Jasmine was the reserve.'

Jordan's eyes again lit on Beatrice's bare shoulders, or perhaps they moved lower this time.

'You could have at least—' she hissed, and then plastered on her official smile as Julius came over with Tobias.

It was then that Beatrice remembered she wasn't wearing a bra. Not that it mattered in terms of the *size* of things, more the ache of things, and the way her body reacted to his presence. She hated how she wanted to leap on him, but of course she just stood there.

'Beatrice.' He gave her an odd half-smile of acknowledgment.

'Your Highness.' Her mouth managed a smile. 'How was your trip?'

'Excellent,' he said. 'Very full-on.'

She should have just smiled and nodded and stopped talking, but Beatrice pushed on. 'I thought Princess Jasmine was the royal patron of the Flower Festival?'

He waited.

'Sir?' she added hastily.

There was an awful silence.

And Beatrice knew she wasn't imagining the awkwardness when Tobias, whose job it was to rescue the Prince from awkward silences, stepped in.

'Sir, I think they're ready for us at the marquee.'

'Of course.'

The group started to walk towards the marquee but she just stood there.

'Beatrice?' said Julius.

'Er...no. I just came to buy some bulbs.'

'I might have a scarf,' Jordan said, scrabbling in her bag.

'I'm really not here to go into the marquee,' Beatrice

insisted. 'I just wanted to see the festival and have a day out…to offer Princess Jasmine my support…'

And it was the wrong thing to say, because they all had to stand there pretending she hadn't just mentioned the missing princess again.

Beatrice didn't know how to be part of a group—she was dreadful at it at the best of times, and obviously she was hopeless now.

'I'll leave you to it, sir.'

'I might just have a quick word with Beatrice regarding…'

She didn't hear regarding what, but whatever excuse Julius had given, Beatrice felt everyone knew it was a lie.

'I wasn't expecting you to be here,' she was very quick to point out.

'I'm aware.'

'What's going on?' Beatrice asked. 'Do they all know?'

'About…?' He frowned and then halted just for a second. 'Actually, please don't answer that. Of course not.'

'So why is it all so awkward?'

'It has nothing to do with you.'

Julius heard his own formal tone and knew it sounded like a put-down when he'd been trying to reassure her. However, there wasn't a hope of any private conversation in the middle of a public festival.

'There were some last-minute changes,' he said.

'Why?'

He halted, and they faced each other a suitable distance apart. She made the mistake of meeting his eyes, clearly believing for a second that she was speaking with Julius the man rather than the Prince.

'What happened to Princess Jasmine? She was supposed to be—'

'Excuse me?' His voice was icily cold. 'Ms Taylor, I

pulled you aside to express polite regret that you've chosen not to join the household on a permanent basis.'

He pulled rank and reminded her very quickly that while they might have shared a bed for all of a few hours, that did not give her access to his life or the private actions of the royal family.

Beatrice knew she should politely nod and leave, but she was truly finding out in the middle of this festival that she was so not cut out for this. Not just the one-night stand game, but this—being spoken to as if there was nothing between them, nor ever had been.

It hurt to be a secret.

She'd been a secret growing up, and she felt the same way now.

To be standing in plain sight and yet not be one of the others—actually, she was less than the others, because she wasn't suitably dressed for the marquee.

Had she stepped off his yacht in a bikini it would have been fine, of course. But not for a member of temporary staff.

Of all the things she hadn't known about life, the worst was this: that when she'd opened herself up it hadn't just made room for joy to flood in, it had also allowed pain to come sweeping in alongside it.

She held onto it now, that pain, and stood with a rictus smile on her lips, for she didn't want it tainting the one glorious night they had shared.

'I hope you enjoy the rest of your afternoon…' Julius said, and gave her his formal public smile.

'I will.'

She nodded, fighting to control herself. His manner was just too reminiscent of the way her mother had dismissed her all those years ago.

All the parts of her she'd held in check, every single hurt and insecurity, came bubbling up, and instead of turning to go bitter words slipped out.

'Not even *one* personal text?'

'We can't be having this conversation,' he told her.

'Why not? You're just talking to your liaison aide.'

'Well, you don't look like one.'

He meant her hair, her dress, the freckles popping off her shoulders, the nipples like studs under the cotton. He was trying to convey all of that right now with his one arch comment, even while he ached to take off her sunglasses so he could better read her expression. But he couldn't do it today.

Beatrice smiled politely and nodded. And then from her sweet lips, and for his ears only, she said the one word you should never say to the next in line to the throne.

It was recognisable in most of the languages she spoke and it began with a B.

Julius's response was supremely polite as he simply nodded.

And Beatrice had never been more grateful for her dark glasses, for it felt as if his eyes were piercing hers, and she could see the anger flickering in his jaw.

'Ms Taylor.'

What had she done?

'Beatrice!' Jordan called out. She had found, of all things, a shawl. 'Esther keeps one in the car...just in case.'

'Jordan...'

'I shouldn't have tried to force you to come.' She directed a pale tentative smile at Beatrice, and it was clear to her that Jordan had been having a nosy little re-read of

Beatrice's file and basic security checks. 'But now you're here…'

Oh, please don't be nice.

She was actually appreciative of the stern doorman who directed her to take off her hat and glasses, and she put the shawl around her shoulders as she stepped into the royal marquee.

Prince Julius was not there to mingle casually with staff and their partners. His back was to her, and Beatrice's back was to him while she stood listening to Esther, who was equally excited to be having a boy as her husband, who was currently walking around with Julius.

'What have you bought?' Jordan asked Beatrice.

'Not much,' she said. 'I'm going to get some tulip bulbs.'

'You've been to the soap stall…' said Jordan.

Julius turned as Jordan inhaled the contents of Beatrice's little paper bag. He was angry, tired, turned on—and something else…

He was worried that the festival was hard for her, and that he had just made it more so.

And why the hell couldn't she have worn grey, as she always did?

Her shoulders were red—they would hurt tonight—and it would seem from the soap Jordan was now waving around that Beatrice had decided to venture away from her usual carbolic.

And that, he acknowledged, put him in the position of being able to understand how she must feel, looking through endless images of him and his dates…

He was cross, too, at her stab about him not texting her except about work—as if she didn't get how hard it had been for him to seem normal this week.

He was suddenly bizarrely tempted to have her removed.

Actually, it wasn't that bizarre, because if anyone else knew the threat she posed to the monarchy then yes, she'd be removed.

Her five-foot-two, pink-shouldered body was a serious threat indeed.

Because if he didn't do the job…

Jasmine couldn't.

This morning's anxiety attack had made that exceptionally clear.

Was he really considering Beatrice as a hetaera?

She was by far too common and his father would refuse.

Then again, so would Beatrice.

He laughed to himself like a mad man at his own thoughts.

'Sir?' Tobias hauled his attention away from yellow-frocked temptation. 'Il Presidente…'

One of his potential fathers-in-law was here, and Julius was always brilliant at small-talk, he reminded himself.

CHAPTER ELEVEN

FIVE DAYS. Just five days.

Her life felt like some dreadful Advent calendar, with no chocolate reward at the end.

She was thoroughly ashamed of herself for the way she'd behaved on Saturday. And at least some of that was because it had showed Julius that she cared.

Maybe she'd had sunstroke. Could she use that as an excuse?

Or she'd tell him she was premenstrual—which she wasn't. But she would be next week. Yes, she'd start banging on about periods and he'd back away. But then again, maybe Julius wouldn't.

Beatrice gave herself the same pep talk she'd give to one of her clients—well, except for the royal client, who didn't want one.

Just carry on as if nothing has happened. And deny, deny, deny, even to yourself, she added, as she pulled on one of her many grey dresses and tied her trainers for the journey into the office.

She bought her coffee, poured it into her new cup, and took the shuttle bus. And then she walked with purpose, fighting not to turn on her phone as she marched along Prince's Lane.

Even the peacocks seemed to know she needed a little

help today, because one was up early this morning, fanning his gorgeous white tail, showing off.

'Thank you,' she told him as she passed, and even turned around to admire him some more.

And then she silently swore as she saw a van make its way to the stables.

Occhi da Cucciolo. Puppy Dog Eyes. It was written in red on the side of the van, surrounded by hearts, and it was driving down the lane. For once it was Beatrice making a panicked call to Jordan, rather than the other way around.

'Jordan, did you approve that puppy and pony photoshoot?'

'Of course not.'

'I've just seen a van on its way to the stables.'

'Oh, no!' She could hear Jordan frantically tapping. 'No, I haven't booked anything.'

'I think…' Beatrice took a breath, remembering the burning she had felt in her soul that night. 'I think I might have messed up.'

'Then get to the stables!' Jordan snapped. 'After the flower festival, believe me, he is in no mood for puppies!'

Beatrice had never run in her life, and refused to do so now, but she did walk *really* fast along the lane, as Jordan barked instructions in her ear.

Normally, she dealt with real crisises with ease, and now she was panicking over some silly puppies.

She was turning into Jordan.

'It's fine.' Beatrice smiled at the bemused woman holding a pale Labrador puppy, and waved at the groomsman, trying to ignore Julius who was on top of his huge black—she glanced down—stallion.

Both man and beast were lathered up, as if they'd been

working hard. The horse's tail was up and he was prancing about and stomping.

The back of the van was open and there were the pups, all in cages, barking and yapping. Of course she'd dealt with it, but it would take more than a few deep breaths to get herself under control.

'If you could take the puppies to the lodge?' Beatrice was all efficient smiles. 'There should be someone to…' To do whatever Jordan could come up with.

'I'll direct them,' one of the stableboys said.

'Do you know how aggressive this horse is?' Julius glared down as he pulled back on the reins. 'What the hell were you thinking?'

'I thought dogs and horses got on…'

Not always, it would seem.

Beatrice stood there, watching as he calmed his excitable horse, with the help of a couple of stable hands, enough that he could finally dismount.

'It was an error,' Beatrice said.

'Oh, and I know when that error occurred.' He glared. 'He would have kicked your puppies across the yard.' He left Beatrice with that horrible vision and addressed the stallion as if he were a toddler. 'And then whose fault would that be, hey?' he asked him, oh, so nicely. 'It would be the same as those irresponsible owners who let their dogs off the leash and then blame you, my poor baby.'

'I'll go,' Beatrice said. 'I'm very—'

'No, no,' he said, with subtle warning. 'You shall wait.'

She stood there, trying to deny her own tension, until finally the stable hands led the beast away, and then he turned and his black eyes were a mix of anger and desire.

'In here,' he said, and marched her into a stable—a very large, airy one that was as immaculate as her newly tidied lounge, but a stable no less.

'Won't they think it odd—?'

'No.'

She swallowed.

'Anything you have to say?' he demanded.

'About the puppies?'

'No, no.' He shook his head. 'For calling me a bastard at a public event.'

'Nobody heard.'

'*I* heard!' He pointed his finger at her and stomped towards her. 'You wanted discretion and for me to ignore you.'

'I did.'

It was dark and very cool in the stable, but he was not.

'Why were you so angry, then, Beatrice?'

'I wasn't angry. Well, a bit…'

'Angry enough to call me a bastard because I didn't text you any personal messages?'

'No, it wasn't about that,' she lied. 'I was more than aware that I wasn't correctly dressed, without you pointing it out.'

'No.' He came right up to her face. 'I said, "You don't look like my liaison aide." How did you not get that? Do you think I would just insult you for no reason?'

'I didn't know.'

'Then you *should* know.'

He sounded insulted, and maybe, yes, from everything Beatrice knew about him she should have known that. She stood still as he lowered his head and inhaled her new fragrant soapy scent.

'You don't smell like my liaison aide either. Are you going to misconstrue *that*?'

'No.'

Great waves of lust seemed to rush towards her with

his every inhalation, as if he pulled the tide in with every breath he took.

'So what happened?' he asked.

'I thought a personal text, perhaps, or that when you called you might—'

'Oh? So you wanted me to ignore Tobias and ask how you felt?'

'No.'

'Did you want me to say, *Are you okay?*' He dropped his voice to a husky whisper, and finally said the words she had craved all week. 'Or to be more considerate with my enquiry. *How are you?* Or, *Speak soon.* Is that what you wanted?'

'No.'

'A personal text, then,' he said. 'A little smiley face. So that when Jordan takes my phone to answer some message from the King she can say, *Ooh, Beatrice is on fire for you*?'

'Of course not.'

She was shaking—not with fear, but with something just as primal. 'Julius, not here...'

'Why not here?'

'Because if anyone came in—'

'You think I'm going to have sex with you in a stable?'

It felt like it. Every atom seemed to crackle. But no, again she'd read him wrong.

'I wouldn't even try, because—believe it or not—I respect my lovers and I would never compromise them.' He was insulted now.

'What do the staff think we're doing in here, then?'

'They'll think that you are being dressed down for your carelessness this morning. It would not enter their heads that I was sleeping with a member of staff. Not for a second.'

'I'm going to go.'

'No, Beatrice. We're going to do something far scarier than sex. We're going to talk.'

'I have to get to work.'

'No, you don't. And if you're asked what took you so long, just tell them, *Prince Julius needed to discuss the events of this morning.* You know how to fob people off—I've watched you do it. Many times!'

He opened the top stable door and light flooded in, but he did not let Beatrice bolt out. Instead he invited her to sit.

'Where?'

'Stand, then.'

He sat on the floor, his back against a wall and his knees up. Finally she joined him, but sitting with her back to the opposite wall and her legs stretched out and crossed at the ankles.

'I have had sex in the stables,' he told her, from a very safe distance.

'Of course you have.'

'But I was young and it was night-time.'

He gave her a brief smile, but then he was serious. 'I've heard the reason you're leaving.' He looked right at her now. 'The security checks?'

'No, it's because we slept together.'

'We hadn't when you turned down the job offer.'

'Come off it, Julius, we were always going to.'

'Fair enough,' he agreed. 'So did the security checks have anything to do with it?'

'No, Jordan just took it that way, and I let her.'

'Only, you *were* upset when you came back from Trebordi.'

'What does it matter?'

'It matters. Come on—you told me about your friend, that you went to look for her but couldn't face it. Now I've heard that when you were nineteen you changed your name from Festa to Taylor.'

'I hated the name Festa. I was named after the festival which they assumed my mother had visited, given…' She waved at her blonde hair. 'I went back and Alicia had gone—the festival too.'

'I'm sorry.'

'I told you—it was my fault we lost touch.'

'I meant about your parents.'

She was silent.

'Look, I can't imagine… I mean, God, my relatives are everywhere. There's one who was born in 1754—you can see him in the Great Hall. He looks like me…'

'Was he a prince?'

'Yes. Bonny Prince Julius, I call him. He's my doppelgänger, but in tights and with a hair ribbon…' He looked at her. 'Have you tried searching for your mother?'

'Why would I?' she lied. 'I think she made her intentions quite clear when she dropped me off at the baby door of the convent.'

'Beatrice, she must have been terrified. I've spoken with some families whose relatives were left at the convent here, and—'

'Please don't,' Beatrice said.

'Did she leave any *segni di ricooscimento*?' he asked.

He clearly had spoken to those families if he knew about signs of recognition.

'I don't want to talk about it.'

'Beatrice, she might have been—'

'Julius, I don't want your take on things. Alicia got gold earrings pinned to her baby suit. I got nothing.' She swallowed down her bitterness. 'I couldn't give a damn about my mother. Can you leave it, please?'

'Fine.'

She went to get up.

'Hey…'

Beatrice took a breath and sat down again.

'I did think of you this week.'

'Julius, I overreacted. I was sunburnt, premenstrual…'

'You should see a doctor,' he said. 'You were dropping tampons only two weeks ago.'

That was true. She'd dropped one on the way to the loo and he'd laughed and picked it up and tossed it to her, like a cricket ball. Then he'd laughed again, because she hadn't been able to catch it.

'I can't progress things between us as normal—you know that,' he told her.

'Of course.'

'I have to marry…'

'Look, I know this can't be love.'

'Of course not.' He dismissed that completely. 'We slept together once…' He pointed out. 'Anyway, I don't do all that.'

'No.'

'I did get you a gift, though—and with great difficulty, believe me. I have asked for an extension before signing the Document of Intent, and once you're finished here I would like to invite you to join me on Regalsi for a week of…'

'Of what?'

'The fun you refuse to have.'

She swallowed.

'Nowhere to run…nowhere to hide. Apparently there are lots of watersports—which I don't like, by the way.'

'No.'

'Why not?'

'You'll be taking your wife there soon.'

'Don't play the moral card here. I don't even know who

my wife is going to be. So my bed isn't out of bounds even though she's going to be in it? But a whole island is?'

He made a rather good point. 'I don't think it's a good idea…' Beatrice attempted.

'So you don't want romance and a week of just us?'

Oh, she did—so badly, but then the agony would be even greater.

'There's no point.'

'There's every point,' he said.

'I don't feel comfortable when the Document of Intent is so close to being signed.'

'It might be weeks. I'm in my father's good books for once. Bizarrely, thanks to you. The dancing and the lack of apology…'

'The trip around the islands,' Beatrice said. 'That was your suggestion. And from everything I heard at the festival you're rather popular. As well as that—'

'A week on a desert island, Beatrice,' he cut in, refusing to be diverted. 'The sand is red. I saw it the morning after we…' He stopped. 'We can get it all out of our systems and hopefully we'll be desperate to escape each other by the end of the week…'

Oh, Beatrice wouldn't be—that much she knew.

'So you're offering me a week of sex?'

He looked at her.

'But no getting closer? No pillow talk…? Of all the rules your parents have put on you, that is the cruellest.'

'Hey!'

Beatrice would not be silenced. 'No, I'm going to say this—'

'You hardly walk around baring your soul.'

'I *choose* not to,' Beatrice said. 'There's a big difference between being private and being forbidden from having friends. Even all these years on, I still think of Alicia, talk to her—' She halted.

'You still speak to her?' he asked. 'In your head?'

'A bit.'

'What would your friend tell you to do?'

She frowned. 'I would *not* be taking advice from Alicia on this,' Beatrice said. 'Her childhood crush was Dante Schininà, and believe me, he was feral. They used to swim in the river together,' she said, 'and then sneak into the cemetery. His mother ran the local brothel—'

'Whoa!' He halted her and then said sulkily, 'Why didn't I get the bad twin?'

Beatrice was saved from answering by the sound of footsteps approaching.

'Think about it,' he said. Then he looked over as the door was pushed open.

It was Jordan.

'There you are,' Jordan said.

Beatrice was simply relieved that Jordan hadn't found them locked in a clinch, or seen her looking dishevelled and mortified.

She would have if Julius hadn't been so restrained. Beatrice was the one without restraint where they were concerned.

'I assume you've heard about the puppies?' Julius said.

'Sir, I don't know what happened with the diary...'

'Beatrice has already apologised,' Julius said. 'I think we can leave it now. Beatrice thinks I possibly might have said I'd do the photoshoot, though I think she might not be remembering very well.'

'Well, Arabella has heard about the puppies...'

'I promised her one if she stopped getting her nanny to do her homework,' Julius explained to Beatrice, and politely he didn't look as she stood up as gracefully as she could.

Beatrice was too discreet to flash her knickers. She stood there, all neat, dusting away sawdust and straw, and hoped she looked suitably chastised for bringing puppies to his precious stables.

Actually, Beatrice was taken aback.

He was supposed to be safe.

Distant.

It wasn't her reputation…it was her heart she was trying to guard. But he already had it. Beatrice knew that now.

'Was he furious?' Jordan asked as they walked back.

'His horse was a bit startled.'

So too was she.

It was a long day, because after the excitement of the morning it was quiet.

All the news about the Prince was upbeat and positive, and it seemed the tide was turning in his favour. Actually, it had already turned—and she knew it. She rather thought the King might know it too. How could he not?

It was so quiet that it left her time to think—about the King crying by the lake, and the Queen pushing his hand away, and a family all grieving the death of a loved one.

And Julius.

Who offered her more than she'd dared even to hope for.

Fun. Adventure. Danger. Passion.

What would Alicia say?

A week on a desert island with the man of your dreams? No strings, just pure bliss?

Beatrice did not need to guess what she'd say.

Go. Have fun. Come on, Beatrice. Do it!

But then she'd fall even more deeply in love with him.

Yes, love.

Not a crush…nor a simple attraction.

She didn't know quite how to define it, but Beatrice was scarily certain that this was love.

It always had been.

From the day he'd breezed in.

Just as he did later that afternoon.

'Here,' he said as he walked into her office. 'All that sulking was for nothing.'

It was the gift he had mentioned. And he'd clearly not just sent Tobias out to grab something—unless Tobias was into gift-wrapping—because it was a small parcel, wrapped exquisitely in red and gold and tied with a beautiful gold silk cord.

'I don't sulk.' She glanced up. 'Well, perhaps a bit.'

She was almost scared to open it…almost wished he'd forgotten her rather than bought her something as lovely as this. And she hadn't even opened it yet!

'Beatrice, I know I have a poor track record, but even at my worst I usually do flowers, or Jordan does…'

'I know. I was just…' She shrugged. 'Sulking.' It sounded safer to admit that than say what was in her heart.

'I learnt from a sultan I knew many years ago not to say I liked anything. If I did, it was immediately wrapped and gifted to me. I almost came home with a cheetah once…'

She smiled. He'd made her smile again even before she'd undone the bow.

'So, I saw this, and I thought how lovely it was. I have no idea what it's worth—please don't pawn it or whatever…it could cause an international incident. Or it might just be a little knick-knack—though I doubt it. Anyway, it was the only way I could get a gift for you. Tobias wanted to log it on the register…'

'What did you tell him?'

'That I'd lost it.'

It was a tiny crystal peacock, with white opals and possibly diamonds in its feathers. Aside from the Prince standing by her desk, it was the most exquisite thing she had seen in her life.

She held it up to the window to let it catch the light, and he stood watching her smile.

'That one doesn't screech.'

'He's beautiful. But...' she shook her head '...I really can't...'

'Oh, I think you can.'

No, she really couldn't. Because then she'd add it to the birthday card he'd signed, which now sat on her dressing table. Another little Julius memento to keep.

'I don't want it.' She put the beautiful creature back into its beautiful box. 'I think it's better that you tell Tobias you found it.'

'Beatrice...'

'Thank you for the thought.'

'It's a gift.'

'Julius, Security do random checks on our bags!'

'They're not going to check *your* bag.'

'Actually, they very often do. And how would I explain that?' She looked at him. 'Or in a week or so, when I leave, how do I go through airport security with the Prince's jewels—?'

'You overthink things.'

'I do,' she agreed. 'That is what I do. I overthink and I overthink, and the more I think about it, the more I don't want him.'

'I saw the way you looked at him—'

'I want something I can dump in the bin a few weeks from now, when this is all a distant memory—not some jewelled peacock glaring at me. So, no thank you to your romantic gesture.'

She knew it was an insult to reject a gift—especially here, especially from the heir to the throne.

'What do you want, Beatrice?'

'I've had what I wanted,' Beatrice told him. 'Our one night. Also, I have thought about it, and I thank you for the invitation, but I will say no to Regalsi.'

'I won't ask twice.'

'If you did the answer would be the same: a flat no. You wanted no strings; I delivered it.'

'Well, you do you, Beatrice,' he said angrily, picking up the gift and pocketing it. 'Blame me, if it helps. Tell yourself I used you, or whatever, but you know that's not true…'

He gave her such a look that even as she stared ahead she felt the burn of his glare.

'You know, perhaps *I* should itemise that night, too…'

Her throat was tight as he brought her pillow talk admissions into her office.

'You got it "over and done with". Got all you wanted.'

'I did.' Beatrice stared coolly back at him. 'Not the martinis, but—'

He didn't even bother to slam the door on his way out.

And his calm exit was a precursor, because for the remainder of the week he blanked her.

Which was incredibly different from being ignored, Beatrice found out.

He was polite, occasionally friendly, often busy—completely normal, in fact. However, Beatrice found out just how precious those glimpses of Julius she'd had before really had been.

The stage curtains had been drawn again, and she had been shut out.

There were no more glimpses, and he no longer chose to make her smile.

Beatrice found out exactly how it felt to be a temp in his household.

CHAPTER TWELVE

'No ONE KNOWS when that day or hour will come—not even the angels in heaven, nor the Son...'

That line had always made Beatrice shiver in church.

Alicia had laughed at her gloom.

Her final day had dawned and she lay there, almost tempted to ring in sick, but knowing she wouldn't.

It wasn't waiting for Jordan's reference that kept her showing up each day.

It was seeing him.

She'd kissed a prince, and instead of turning into a frog he'd stayed a prince. He'd stayed exactly who he was.

It was Beatrice who had changed. She'd been changing since they met, coming into herself in the weeks she'd been at the palace.

And it was killing her to leave.

She got through the Friday morning meeting, and the mood was a little jubilant, even, as it concluded. The Prince's trip had gone well, there had been a whole week without drama since, and his appearance at the Flower Festival had been a hit.

And not a single apology had been made on the Prince's behalf in the three months she had been here.

His single transgression Beatrice would certainly not be mentioning, because of course it was also her own, so she smiled and accepted congratulations for the newly whole-some Prince Julius and the PR triumph she had brought about.

'So what's next for you?' Despina asked as Beatrice slipped on her jacket.

'I'm mid-interviews,' Beatrice said with a wavering hand. 'We'll see.'

'Well, if the whispers are true...' Despina smiled.

Beatrice gave nothing away, but, yes, there was an exceptionally exciting role for which she was applying. She would be needing a very glowing reference from Jordan, and there would be extensive security checks...

Julius was the reason she couldn't stay. It had never been about her past.

This was not love. She'd been told that by the man himself. And, after all, what would she know about that? But whatever it was—love or infatuation—it was enough that she had no choice but to leave.

She walked through the Great Hall and went to take the stairs, but then she paused, for there was a portrait of Julius. Only, it wasn't his drop-dead good looks that halted her in her tracks.

The King had stood here when she'd seen him. Staring up at his youngest son. She'd assumed it was a portrait of Claude—from the King's stance she'd assumed grief or anguish...

'Are you coming?' Despina called.

'Of course,' Beatrice said, and took the passageway that led towards Julius's residence. It was bright, with the sun refusing to admit it was the end of summer, denying it as it shone fiercely, dispersing the tiny puffs of white cloud drifting above the glittering ocean.

Bellanisiá was looking exceptionally beautiful this morning.

Despite her smiles, and her seemingly easy chat with a colleague, it was killing her to leave.

'Ooh…' Despina said, halting and looking down on the central courtyard.

'What?'

'I'm not sure…' She took out her phone. 'Maybe nothing, but it looks like Princess Jasmine's arriving.'

Beatrice frowned. Jasmine was often here, but she looked down and saw that she wore a silver robe and a diadem.

'She must have been summoned,' Despina told her.

'Because she missed the festival?'

'No.' Despina shook her head. 'This looks official.'

She was firing off texts and reading replies, and Beatrice now saw there were three men in robes walking at a pace across the courtyard.

'Queen's Teiria has left her residence too…'

There really was something happening.

'It must be something serious,' Despina said. 'A death, perhaps…'

'Or a wedding?' Beatrice croaked.

'No.' Despina shook her head. 'They wouldn't be calling the Princess in for that. Oh, my goodness—this is what happened when Prince Claude died. What if the King—?'

Beatrice turned and saw Julius, walking with Tobias beside him. Of course he blanked her. Well, he was hardly going to stop and fill her in.

His face was so grey. And, terrible person that she was, now that she'd seen he was okay Beatrice was rather hoping for a funeral instead of a wedding. But, for her sins, she knew it must be otherwise.

'Let's watch…' Despina said once they'd passed.

'I have to get back,' Beatrice said.

Beatrice wanted to be sick as she fled to the offices,

only to find quiet chaos there. Jordan was opening a cup-board and taking a jacket out of a suit holder—clearly one she kept there for just this kind of day.

'I was in the loo,' Jordan said, changing her earrings and her shoes at the same time and almost falling over.

'What is it?' Beatrice asked, still guiltily hoping that Despina was right and she herself was wrong.

'The scribes have been summoned…and the priests and masters…' Jordan held on to the desk. 'The Docu-ment of Intent.'

Clearly not even Jordan had known.

'Now?' Beatrice checked.

'Tobias just called…' someone said. 'Prince Julius has asked for a closed room.'

'So, not right now?' Beatrice checked, because, oh, she wanted to be gone so badly. She wanted this to take place on Monday, or tomorrow, or at least a few hours from now…

Surely he could have done that for her? Just that? No dates, or dinners, or peacocks, or trips to Regalsi. Her only stipulation had been discretion.

She shouldn't have had to specify that she didn't want to be here when the announcement was made, should she?

'They'll be thrashing out dates and things,' Jordan said. 'I'd better go.' She gave Beatrice a little pat. 'Well done. Looks like he's changed his spots after all…'

To all intents and purposes…

Except he wasn't a leopard; he was a lovely panther, and that was that.

It was the most awful wait. She felt as if she was watch-ing the Vatican for smoke as she looked out on the palace, but there was nothing.

Well, Princess Jasmine had left, and the Queen had gone to her private apartments, but still nothing…

For hours.

She went into her office, just to escape it all, and then finally Jordan returned.

Beatrice looked up as she knocked and came in. 'Some last day!' Jordan said, and her cheerful greeting sounded a touch forced.

'Is it done?' Beatrice asked. 'Has he signed?'

'Hmm...' She gave a little hand gesture. 'They're meeting again at seven.'

'Is that usual?'

'I remember Prince Claude dragged it out. It's all politics now.' Jordan shrugged. 'I've heard there's to be a formal announcement on Monday, but my guess is we'll know tonight.'

'I won't.'

'Stay, then.'

'Ooh, I don't think I'd make a good wedding planner...'

'True.' Jordan smiled, only it didn't quite meet her eyes. *Be subtle*, Beatrice reminded herself. 'Are you excited?'

'Very!' Jordan nodded.

'So, do the Queen and the Princess return for the signing?'

'No.' Jordan shook her head and went to the little window, looked out on Beatrice's dreary semi-basement view.

Beatrice was certain that Julius's very loyal PA was very, very upset and trying hard not to be.

'So they just have to be there for the announcement?' Beatrice asked. 'Only, Despina said—'

'What would Despina know?' Jordan snapped.

'I think she was worried something dreadful must have happened. Like with—' She halted, as everyone did rather than say Prince Claude's name.

'I guess...' Jordan had recovered. 'No, it was just...'

She pulled away from the window. 'Times are changing, perhaps.'

Or the King was showing Julius his hand.

What had Julius told her about his father's latest turn of phrase 'progressing the monarchy'? Was he threatening Julius with the line of succession?

But Julius didn't object to a woman ruling. He was, Beatrice was completely sure, simply giving his sister the privacy she craved.

'I'm going up…' Jordan pushed out another smile.

'I might go and have something to eat.' Beatrice replied.

'Do,' Jordan said. 'Then I must take your computer and phone… Like I said…some last day!'

'Yes.'

Some last day.

The lid of her new cup leaked. Beatrice found that out when she dripped coffee down herself as she sat by the lake. Then she felt a sudden frantic panic, because there were just six little cygnets today.

She cast her eyes around for the lazy one…

She couldn't see him anywhere.

The worst ever last day.

'Beatrice.'

He said her name and she closed her eyes rather than look at him. She was sitting with a very cold coffee and just a few hours left on the clock, but she was determined to see it through.

'I thought we were ignoring each other.'

'Well, I'm expected to wish you farewell.'

'Farewell, sir.'

'How's the new cup?'

'Disappointing,' she said as he took a seat by her side. Then, 'You couldn't wait till I'd gone?'

'I asked earlier in the week for more time. I thought I had it.'

'Well, clearly you didn't ask forcefully enough.'

But Julius was kind. She knew that. He wouldn't put her through this if he had a choice.

'Beatrice, I was conceived in case my brother died. I'm not complaining. I'm hardly a lamb being led to the slaughter.'

'So you want this?'

'It's not about what I want. It's about duty. It's about what's best for the country. I'm crazy about you, Beatrice, and you know it. Hell, my doctor even wants to take blood to see why I'm losing weight.'

She frowned.

'I was fine with it all until a few weeks ago...*almost* fine,' he amended. 'And then they had to hire someone to fix my image. To fix me...' He gave her a black smile. 'Please listen. I can give you one week, and I will do everything in that week to make up for the years you've hidden yourself away.'

'I haven't hidden myself away.'

'You know you have. Please, just think about it. Now you're finished here...'

'I'm not going away with a man who's signed the Document of Intent—whatever the hell that even means.' She stared ahead and spoke calmly, but her words were final. 'Delay signing and then we'll speak.'

'That's not an option.'

'What could he possibly do to you?'

'The *"he"* you refer to is the King?'

'You hold all the cards,' Beatrice said. 'It's not as if he's got many other options. He's not going to change the line of succession.'

Jasmine couldn't even make a speech at a festival. She wasn't an option here.

'We're not having this conversation.'

'I'm right.'

'Beatrice, I have always known that I was to marry. With privilege—'

'Comes responsibility,' she cut in. 'Blah-blah-blah.' She stared at him. 'I've been passed up for better than you, Julius.'

'What are you talking about?'

'Him!' She pointed skywards. 'My mother chose Him over me.' She stared at the six little swans, all happily swimming with one missing. 'I lied. I found out who my mother is when I was nineteen. She was a nun at the convent...'

'A nun?'

'Well, not when I was conceived,' Beatrice said. 'She was pregnant when she entered the convent as a novice, and I was popped into that baby box without a second thought.'

'You don't know that—'

'I do. She told me herself. Well, in as many words. I went back when I was nineteen to find Alicia, to find out if my mother had left anything to identify herself or me, and I found out the truth then. Eventually. I was a little blonde version of Sister Catherine, so I was sent to Milan, and then Switzerland. I thought it was because I was so good at languages, but really it was to get me away.'

'They all knew?'

'No. Reverend Mother guessed when I was ten or so.' She looked at him. 'Sister Catherine taught me Latin, and she made me go and play outside when I asked if I could stay in at playtime.'

'No favourites?' he said, and she knew he recalled their conversation.

'Not even her daughter. Believe me, she wasn't sneaking cuddles. She abandoned me as a baby and then sent me away at eleven. But she gave me away every day in between. I was screaming with nightmares, dreaming I was running through the fair at night, and all that time she was only a step away. So I know about duty, and what it means to protect a secret.'

He closed his eyes.

'I'm not asking for marriage,' she told him. 'I know that's impossible. But I won't sneak into your suite via a tunnel, nor be hidden away on an island or ignored in plain sight.'

'What, then?'

'I don't know,' Beatrice admitted. 'I don't think it even matters what I say. You'll keep on protecting the Princess, shielding her, and to hell with everyone else.'

'My sister needs to live a quiet life,' he admitted. 'We always agreed that if anything happened to my brother I would step in.'

'And you have stepped in,' she said. 'And you have stepped up. Just not when it comes to me.' She stared at him then, and still did not raise her voice. She would not cry, but she would tell him a truth. 'Do you know, I really think it is love?' Beatrice said. 'Because it hurts just as much.'

'Don't even compare—'

'Yes,' Beatrice said, 'I do compare it. I'm a tricky secret. Well, you don't have to worry any more. Go and do your duty, Prince Julius. To your country and to the people you love...'

'He's King...'

'And clearly you're not.'

It was mean, and it was cold, but to hell with it all.

'You can be so—'

'Yes, I can,' she cut in. 'That's why you hired me.'

'No,' he said, 'it isn't.'

Julius looked at her in her perpetual grey and thought of the fresh air she had breezed into his life, and how the best bit of his day was making Beatrice smile.

He could see her eyes flashing tears, but still she would not cry, and he hated it that she couldn't.

Wouldn't.

He had left Jasmine sobbing, his mother weeping and reminding him of the promise made, and yet Beatrice's pinched, angry face and her refusal to bring it all to the table hollowed him.

'You don't know the half of it, Beatrice.'

'Perhaps not,' she said.

He knew he could never discuss the hold his father had on him—not to a temporary employee, nor to a lover.

'Then again,' Beatrice said, 'you'll never know even the half of me.'

He saw she was done.

'Good luck.' She gave him a smile as she tipped her cold coffee onto the ground. 'I might see you at my leaving party.'

'You won't.'

He stood, and therefore so did she.

'Sir,' she said.

And for all the world, if anyone were watching, they would think he was thanking her for a job well done.

All the passion only he saw and felt was just for him, he knew, and he watched her walk off as if nothing had occurred. She even waved to Tobias as she passed by.

Ever polite, Tobias halted, then he smiled and shook her hand, and wished her well before coming over to him.

'Sir,' he said, 'the Queen has requested lunch, and Princess Jasmine has asked that you call her urgently—'

'Tobias,' he cut in, 'they'll have to wait.'

CHAPTER THIRTEEN

DUTY FIRST.

Yes, he might have coloured outside the lines sometimes, but Julius loved his country. And now, on this most important of days, he'd left it behind.

Julius was approaching Trebordi from the sky.

Three jagged cliffs fell away to the ocean, so sharply it was as if they sliced like a hot knife through butter. Certainly, their slicing was a lot neater than Beatrice with a cake knife!

It was a beautiful, brutal place. Even in summer the wind meant a rather careful approach for the helicopter was required.

He saw the convent as they swept past it, and the hilly walk from there to the village. He saw the church, the cemetery, and he glimpsed a little of the life she had lived. This woman he might never see again.

The chopper came down on a dark flat area cut out from the trees—a scar on the very beautiful landscape.

'I don't know how long I'll be,' he said to Tobias, and took off his headphones.

'Sir.'

He felt the gravel crunch beneath his feet. This was the place where Beatrice Festa had been told she was born. He walked around, kicking a few stones. In truth, he didn't know what he was doing there…knew simply that he needed to think.

He walked through the village, garnering a few looks, but the people soon went back to their coffees—and he really didn't care.

The church was gorgeous, with rice and confetti between the stones outside. There must have been a wedding recently, but apart from that there was nothing. No answers here.

He could hardly ask the lady passing with her dog for directions to the local brothel! Or could he? For that was where Dante's mother had worked, he remembered.

Julius thought of how cross Beatrice had been with her little wild friend who'd swum in the river and roamed the cemetery, so he wandered there, opening the latch, grateful for the shade and the soft silence.

He saw all the family plots, including the Schininàs, but there were no Festas, of course.

No wonder she had been so jealous of those earrings… those little pieces of gold her friend's mother had left.

But her mother must have been terrified, even if Beatrice was convinced she had felt nothing.

Then a spray of frangipani caught his eye. Placed on a single grave, away from the others. No, not a spray, but a wedding bouquet, the waxy flowers yellowing at the edges.

Schininà.

He looked at the dates and the inscription and wondered if this was Dante's mother. Carmella had been buried away from the rest of her family, it would seem.

He moved the bouquet, its scent still lingering as he lifted it, and saw the names on the little tag that held the bouquet together.

Dante and Alicia

Beatrice had been here just a couple of weeks ago.

A breath away from finding her friend.

'Best left,' Beatrice had said.

Had she been protecting her mother by not asking around? Surely she could have found her friend if she really cared? It had taken him mere minutes...

Instead Beatrice had changed her name, cut herself off from the one person she had ever loved...

Taylor... Tailor...

He thought back to his hated Latin. *I cut.*

Her new name was no accident.

He replaced the bouquet and walked up to the convent. He looked at the little school attached to it, and could not fathom cutting himself off from his sister or brother.

They'd argued, they'd rowed, but he would kill for them...

Marry for them?

Julius soon found what he was looking for—an iron door in the wall, beneath it an inscription with the name of its benefactor.

The baby door.

At home the convent had a wheel, but here it was a door.

He pulled it open and peered inside, and he was certain that Beatrice must have done the same.

A part of him wished there had been time to tell her more of what he knew from his visits to Di Dio Bellanisiá; that there he had met families and heard of their pain and endless guilt...

'Signor?'

He turned and looked down at a nun.

'It's not a toy,' she scolded.

'Scusi,' Julius said.

And he understood now why they had moved her to Milan. Because a brown-eyed Beatrice was looking up at him. He saw a little pointed nose and tight lips, a slight figure, so similar, and yet... She was like a waxwork, or a dead fish lying on the deck of a boat, with nothing behind her velvet brown eyes.

Nothing of passion and terror and shame. None of the things that made you question yourself at times. That caused you to doubt and ponder and consider or regret.

'The bell on the door rings and interrupts us. Always tourists!' She sneered a little. 'Please, show some respect.'

'Of course. It's a beautiful convent.' He looked up at the stunning Sicilian Baroque-style building, but she gave nothing back. 'Is it seventeenth century?' he asked.

'There are tours on the first Friday of the month.'

'I was just thinking...'

Julius peered at the black iron. Julius was good at small talk—well, unless any sunburned shoulders were around. He could usually engage anyone. But Sister Catherine was not here to talk.

'How lucky—' he began.

'We take care of the babies.'

'No, no.' He halted her tersely. 'I meant, how lucky I am.'

She looked at his smart clothes. 'You clearly have a privileged life, *signor*,' she said, and pointed to the donation box above the baby door.

This woman rejected conversation.

Beatrice deflected.

This woman rejected the chance to tell a tourist a little about the beautiful building. She rejected that little moment of connection. She rejected it coldly, and had done the same to her daughter in every minute of her childhood.

But to find out that this was your mother...?

No wonder Beatrice hadn't been able to walk down

that hill, or pick up the phone. Even he felt the cold snub of this nun.

He wanted to say something cutting. He wanted to call her out so he could savour the moment, relish it later, let her know the pain she had caused.

He chose not to, for it was not his place.

Furthermore, he doubted this woman would care.

'Yes, Sister,' he said. 'I am privileged indeed.'

He was loved by someone who, thanks to this woman, barely dared to love anyone.

'Good afternoon,' he said, and although he wanted to add *Sister Catherine*—because he wanted to see her give that little jolt as she realised he knew her name—he stopped himself.

That was not the person he wanted to be.

He turned and left.

Julius stood on the headland and looked out to sea. He wished he could speak to his brother.

And then he paused.

No one could make this choice for him.

So he watched as the woman closed up the baby door, as she had done some twenty-nine years ago, and walked away without so much as a glance.

No, he didn't need his brother, nor his advice.

And he knew, as he had told Beatrice so recently, that with privilege came responsibility. Only there was no blah-blah-blah to it…

He smiled.

His choice was already made.

CHAPTER FOURTEEN

'ANY NEWS?' Beatrice asked when Jordan called her to come up.

'No. Julius is off somewhere with Tobias. He'll be back for the signing.' Jordan was, as always, practical. 'It's just security stuff I want you for. I need your computer.'

'Oh...' Beatrice nodded. 'Of course.'

'And your phone, plus lanyard, ID...'

'Sure.'

Beatrice took out all the items and stared at the phone for a very long moment.

She hated her parting shot to him.

Hated that she'd had to get in first...strike first.

For all her bravado, they had slept together once and never been on a date... He was hardly going to turn his back on duty or throw his sister under the bus for that.

Yet he had made her smile, had made her feel so happy and wanted. And as much as he'd been able to, he had offered her more than one night.

Could she fire off a quick text to him? What would she say? Sorry? Good luck? And what for?

Her phone would be checked—and anyway, in the grand scheme of a kingdom, what did feelings even matter?

'Beatrice!' Jordan called.

The team was gathering, and she hadn't expected anyone to come. It was a very rushed leaving do, given the events of the day, and it touched her very much the effort Jordan had gone to.

'Unfortunately Prince Julius can't be here, or Tobias, or...'

It was quite a low turn-out, Beatrice saw, but there was some good news at least.

'I was annoyed you were leaving,' Jordan continued, 'so you were only going to get a temp's gift. But Julius—*Prince* Julius,' she corrected, 'said I was being petty.'

Beatrice smiled and opened the velvet box. Clearly Jordan had chosen the gift, because it was a lovely gold bracelet.

Jordan helped her put it on her wrist. Beatrice knew there were no antihistamines in her bag, but she must have turned into a nicer person—because she didn't tell them she was allergic to gold, just smiled and said thank you.

There were also two cards.

'I might open these later,' Beatrice said, but immediately gave in and started slicing them open.

She smiled at all the lovely messages, and there was Jordan's private phone number.

'Keep in touch,' Jordan said.

'I'd love to.'

Tobias had signed it too, and wished her well, and she found she was looking forward to hearing about his baby boy.

Wow, she was almost crying—not that Beatrice showed it.

And then she opened the official card.

It was very bland, but then Julius chose to be bland when he did not want others to know his feelings. It was cream, with his insignia on it, and inside there was a typed message thanking her for her service. And his signature.

She checked the back of the card.

Surely a teeny little smile or something…?

She peered into the envelope.

'There's no money in there,' Jordan said, smiling.

'Pity!' she quipped.

And that was it.

'You'll need this for the shuttle bus,' Jordan said, as she handed her a temporary pass after everyone had wandered off. 'And I'm really sorry to have to do this but—'

'It's fine.'

Jordan went through her bag, and it was perhaps just as well she'd known she would, or she might have pinched the top of his whisky decanter, or something equally dreadful.

There was no little peacock lurking in there, either.

'It's been a pleasure, Beatrice,' Jordan told her.

'It's been interesting!' Beatrice smiled. 'Wish the Prince well for me.'

That was all she could do.

Followed by a hug and a wave as she walked away.

Really, she'd barely been there any time at all, and yet it hurt so much to leave.

More than it ever had to leave anywhere.

Even when she had left the convent at eleven it had only been one person she'd wept for.

Now it was for love, and people, and her little home on the marina, and lakes and swans…

But there would be no final lingering there—no frantic check for the lost cygnet. Because a flash of silver caught her eye. Jasmine was coming out of the rose garden and walking towards the lake.

Beatrice changed direction and walked down the tree-lined avenue, but she kept wanting to turn and look at this woman who wanted a quiet life. And who could blame her?

Not Beatrice.

Who could blame Julius for protecting someone he loved and honouring a promise?

Clearly, you're not, she had sneered at him when he had spoken of the King.

What a horrible woman she was. And what a wonderful king he would be.

She had just wanted some time. And his father wanted a wedding *now*.

His father… Who had stood there weeping…

Perhaps he thought a wedding might somehow bring back his son, rectify things… Might pull Julius into line.

Good luck, she thought. Because even at their first meeting—before all of this—Beatrice had known he was his own man. No prodigal son returning with his head down was he… Julius had returned ready for duty.

The King might be threatening the line of succession—Beatrice could see that clearly now—but it made no sense. He loved his son. That much she could also see. She had seen it in the photos she had looked at, and in the way he had stood there staring at his portrait.

He loved Julius.

How could he not?

And then it dawned on her.

The King was trying to soothe the fretful Queen, who had lost one child and was terrified of losing another.

Oh, Julius.

She was going to be nicer and kinder, Beatrice vowed. No more sex with men who didn't want anything more than that from her.

Only, that wasn't fair.

How she hated it that it had ended like this.

She hated it so much that she couldn't let it.

She was like a ship on its final voyage. A ship that didn't quite know how to bring itself into port.

And even as she made the vow it was tested. Because she'd caught a glimpse of those secret gates to the tunnel beyond and she couldn't help but peek. One look at his secret tunnel, she decided, and wrenched open the heavy door.

It wasn't a velvet tunnel after all.

It was awful bricks and a fluorescent light that flicked on automatically.

And an intercom.

Beatrice buzzed because it was there and because she couldn't help herself.

But she got no response.

So she buzzed again, and again, and again.

He's out, she reminded herself... *Go home, Beatrice.*

But she'd walked away from Alicia, and she could not have the only two relationships in the world she cared about end on such terrible terms.

Even if he told her what she could do with her apology at least she would have made it. Told him how much better he had made her world.

So she buzzed again.

And she would keep buzzing...

Or maybe she should write a note—just a quick *sorry* and fling it under the door. But the door was awfully heavy and there were no gaps she could see.

Would he even come down here?

Stop overthinking, Beatrice thought, and took out her journal.

But then she heard the crackle of the intercom and braced herself for a curious servant—or perhaps Jordan dealt with this sort of thing... Or did Tobias deal with all those women in ball gowns?

'What?' Julius's voice was clipped and angry and she didn't care.

'It's Beatrice.'

'What do you want, Beatrice?'

'I don't know…the chance to apologise.'

He was silent.

'You will be a brilliant king and… Can I come up?'

There was a long silence, and just when she was sure he would never reply, suddenly the internal door clicked.

Beatrice pushed it open and peered in.

There was still no velvet, just more lights and brick walls, and now she walked where angels would never dare: beneath the palace to his lair.

She should be ashamed, really, but she found she was elated instead at having a second chance for a better goodbye…

Julius released the door and inhaled. He did not need this now. Not now, when he needed every part of his brain focussed.

But the best-laid plans… Beatrice certainly knew how to lay them to rest! The whole country was under her five-foot-two threat!

So he used the ten or so minutes her walk would take to prepare himself for her arrival, and then gave himself a stern talking-to in the mirror.

Do not engage.

He nodded to himself.

Politely ask her to wait.

This decision was his alone. By far too much to land on Beatrice. She must have no clue until it was done.

But then came a knock at his very private door, and in came his moody former liaison aide, blinking like a mole coming up onto a lawn.

* * *

'Gosh!' she said, and didn't try to hide the effect he had on her. 'Look at you!'

He wore full dress uniform, but she was up close this time and could really admire the deep grey and Prussian blue belted coat and boots.

'You're going out?' she asked.

'Clearly. I have a meeting. I need to leave in a couple of moments,' he snapped. 'So be fast.'

'I apologise. I was incredibly mean before—'

'What's new?'

'I would like that week on Regalsi, if it's still available. Even a couple of days if that's all you can manage.'

'You're so fickle.'

'Not usually,' Beatrice said. 'But, yes, sometimes I am.'

'What do you want to do with our time there?'

'Have fun.'

'I thought "fun" was what you wanted the night we made love.'

'We had sex, Julius,' she corrected him, using his own words, 'and you're right. I'm dreadful at fun. I don't want to be, though. I'd like some time on Regalsi with you and hopefully to leave on better terms.'

'We'll talk in a bit.'

She swallowed. 'Fine...' Deflated, she watched him check his reflection. 'I thought I'd like a one-night stand...' she said.

'You didn't like it?'

'I liked it too much,' she said, smiling, 'and then I had to go and spoil it all by wanting more.'

'More?' he checked.

'I've never done this before. I don't tend to get involved...' he wasn't making this easy '...with anyone.'

'Why?'

'Don't you have to go…?'

'Why don't you get involved with anyone?'

'I'm terrified they might not like me back.' She saw he was watching her in the mirror. 'And I'm scared that I'm cold and unfeeling like my mother.'

'You're not like her.'

'You don't know that.'

'Beatrice, there are seven swans a-swimming tonight…'

'Are there? I couldn't go over to check… Jasmine was there…' She swallowed. 'I understand that you have to protect her.'

'We can't discuss that,' Julius said.

'No.' She nodded. 'We're only about fun!' She wanted to be fun, and so she moved to wrap her arms around his neck. 'Can you bring this uniform to Regalsi?'

'Beatrice,' he said firmly, uncoiling her arms, 'I do have to go. However, you *are* very nice,' he told her. 'And I like sitting on the bench with you.'

'Thank you.'

'Believe it or not, you're getting off lightly. I'm sure you'd hate being Queen Consort.'

'I'll have you know I'd be brilliant.'

'And at being a hetaera?'

'Sitting at your knee and gazing up at you?' She shook her head. 'No, thanks. But I will be your lover for the next few nights.'

'Really?'

'Yes.'

'And then walk away?'

'Absolutely!'

He smiled. 'Did you like your leaving present?'

She held up her wrist. 'It was very thoughtless of you; I'll be covered in welts soon.' She looked at her wrist. 'But thank you. I do like it—very much.'

'No welts,' he told her. 'We only do the good stuff here. It's nickel you're allergic to.'

'Hmm...'

'So doubting,' he said. 'I really do have to go. But there's some food coming up. It will be in the butler's kitchen. Help yourself. He'll buzz. Wait till he's gone before you collect it. Don't answer any calls.'

'I know.'

'I mean it.'

'Yes.' She watched him go. 'Good luck.'

'You don't mean that,' he said.

'I do. You have to protect the people you love, and I get that.'

'You do?'

'Yes, believe it or not, I actually do. I hope you get a wonderful wife.'

'I hope so too. But there's no luck required if you're adequately prepared.' He looked at her for a long moment. 'Thank you for going against all your principles and coming in through the tunnel.'

He had to go—he mustn't keep the King waiting. Especially tonight! However, he looked at Beatrice one last time. She was still pretending to be fun, while sitting glumly on the bed.

'Hey, I found out something,' he told her.

'What?'

'I looked up that guy—the feral one, Dante Schininà. He's done well for himself.'

'Please don't.'

'Okay,' he said. 'Anyway, I really have to go.'

'You really found Dante?'

'I found out he owns a hotel in Ortigia, Sicily.' He gave her a smile. 'I'm going to be a while.'

* * *

'I know you are.' She watched him put on his cap. 'Julius, can I say one thing? Not as me, but as the person you hired?'

'You can't come to the meeting with me.'

'Of course not.' She took a breath, because she knew there were things he could not tell her—she very much understood that now. She looked at him, and knew he did not need her going for the jugular, as she usually did. 'Actually, I'll just say it being me.'

'Very well.'

'I don't have a family, but you do...'

He gave a small mirthless laugh.

'Your father is grieving...'

'Yes—grieving the fact it wasn't me that died.' He gave her a look that told her he didn't have time for this. 'Beatrice, I have to go.'

'Julius, that book Jordan lent you...'

He picked up his sword and sheathed it in the scabbard on his left-hand side. He was clearly not going to make small talk now.

'Who does a king talk to?' Beatrice asked.

'Not his son, that's for sure.' He gave her a grim smile. 'What happened to Fun Beatrice?'

He was right; she was incapable of being bubbly for even five minutes. 'Good luck,' she said.

She didn't mean it.

Hopefully they'd choose him a horrible wife...

She was a dreadful person.

She walked out onto the terrace and breathed in the fragrant air.

She knew the slippery slope she was on.

A holiday—a week with him in paradise.

And then he'd head off and marry, because he had to,

and he'd have dark-eyed babies, and he'd love them, and Beatrice knew she would have to watch from afar.

She knew she couldn't be kept at a distance all over again.

And so she decided to be happy.

Tonight.

She went into the shower and looked at her hair, which was straggly. She stripped off and stood under the lovely strong jets.

She was heartbroken, but she was living. She was in love with someone who didn't do all that, but she would have her week with him and that would be that.

Yes.

No.

Yes!

The buzzer rang and she waited for the butler to leave before she padded out into the kitchen. It wasn't food. It was four Birthday Girl Martinis. She smiled that he could be so thoughtful. There were chocolates too, and another present. A new coffee cup from the palace souvenir shop.

Wrapped in a towel, she sat on a very smart chair and found out that he was right. Alicia had always been impossible to find online, but it took two minutes for her to find Dante. Indeed, that grubby little boy her friend had adored was now the owner of an extremely luxurious hotel in Ortigia—a very beautiful part of Sicily. Dante had done very well for himself.

It took two of the very sweet martinis before she could further look up the hotel in Ortigia and find out what she could about the owner. And then the world stopped spinning as she saw her friend smiling back at her.

Alicia and Dante.

She had missed their wedding in Trebordi by a few days…

Tears spilled from her eyes. Because had she dared to walk up that hill then she'd have heard the gossip and found Alicia…

Julius met Jordan in the Great Hall.

'I believe the King and Queen are ready to receive you, sir.'

'Thank you.' He nodded.

'Jordan, can I speak with you afterwards?'

'Of course, sir.'

It was a very long walk to the throne room, past the portraits. He paused at a couple, because amongst the dour faces were a few eyes that smiled, and it was nice to have a few rebels to relate to. And there was Bonny Prince Julius—smiling in his tights and curls…

He'd always felt burdened by his history, the traditions, the faces that stared down from the walls, some oddly familiar in their similarity to his own.

Imagine having no one.

Imagine growing up without a thread of identity.

And then finding out the one thread you had was poison…

As always, his thoughts went back to the woman who had made it through this world for the most part alone. Finding out what her mother had done, knowing that the pain he was causing her might compare to that, had stunned him.

And that was when he had known it was love.

A very inconvenient love, as far as the palace was concerned.

An impossible love, but one worth fighting for.

And that meant being prepared to lose—possibly to hurt others, to inconvenience many. But he would do what he could because… He could not justify it logically, for it went against everything he had been taught, but Julius knew he was right.

If not, the King would be forced to choose.

'Your Majesties,' Julius greeted his parents. 'Could I ask for a closed room?'

'No,' his father said. 'There have already been too many delays, too many negotiations. It's time to proceed.'

'Then I must formally request my titles be put into abeyance.'

'Wait—' the King instructed the scribe, and Julius watched Phillipe's eyes bulge.

'No,' Julius said, 'this is a formal request. Please note it.' He looked at the chief scribe. 'And then we shall either proceed with all present or in a closed room.'

'Proceed,' the King said, challenging him to continue with all present.

'Very well. I will not be signing the Document of Intent. I will choose my own partner, when and if I am ready, and when and if they agree.'

'"They"?' his father checked. 'Are you gay?'

'I could be.'

'Julius!' his mother exclaimed. 'Enough!'

He looked to his mother and could hear the frantic plea in her rather too high voice.

'I request a closed room,' she said.

It took for ever to clear it.

'You promised...' the King began.

'Yes,' Julius said, 'I did. But we are all older now, and your daughter is stronger than you allow for. I have spoken at length with Princess Jasmine and she is prepared to take over my duties. I, of course, have offered her my full support.'

'No. She can't do it,' said his father.

'I disagree. She will be wise and gentle. As well as that,

she has a husband who, although he would prefer to stay out of the spotlight, will stand by her side when he has to. And I will stand by the other. Anyway, we've spoken. It's done.' He looked at his father. 'You wanted Claude to be your heir. We all did. But he's gone. You have a son willing to take his place—'

'With conditions.'

'With one condition,' Julius corrected. 'And if you cannot agree to that, then you have and a daughter who, though she would prefer to quietly raise her family, is prepared to step up for what is right. But you are King. You make the rules. For now,' he ominously added.

'Respect…' his father warned.

'Of course. But don't raise your children to be rulers and then expect them to sit meekly by while you dictate their futures. You have heirs—a prince and a princess. In the blink of an eye we could all be ruled by Arabella, who would be a very strong queen. Think on that when you make your decision.'

'You always have to get your way…'

'Perhaps you taught me too well.'

Julius walked over to his father, who did not flinch, and neither did he expect him to.

'Claude, like you, was born to be King,' Julius said. 'And you made sure he was ready for all that lay ahead. Jasmine never wanted it, and you made sure she never had to shoulder that burden. So you had your spare…' He looked at his father. 'A natural leader.'

'Arrogant.'

'Like father, like son.' He stared at the King. 'You should know better than to try to bring me to heel.' He looked right at his father, 'So it's up to you to choose what is best for your country and for your family. And may I say you have two excellent choices. Some rulers have none.'

'You dare walk out on your King!'

He dared. But then he heard his mother's urgent plea. 'Cenzo...'

She called the King by his given name and Julius stilled.

'Please...' she begged her husband. 'Stop this from happening.'

'Jasmine needs a quiet life,' his father asserted.

Julius turned, and he saw then the strain his father was under, how he had changed so much in a year that suddenly Julius didn't recognise him. Outwardly, he was the same—grumpy and stern—but they had smiled together before. Laughed, even.

Beatrice was right. Who did his father have to confide in? For his mother was still crumbling under the weight of grief—that much Julius could see.

'She couldn't even manage the Flower Festival!' the King shouted.

'Then why the hell would you put this on her?' Julius stared at his father. 'Do it if you must, but it's on you.' Julius turned to his mother. 'And on you too. You push and you push for this wedding to take the pressure off Jasmine, and yet you burden her with your doubt. But she is strong. You know she doesn't want this, but she is standing by me and she supports my decision. Talk to your husband.'

'Julius...'

He was done. 'I'm taking tonight off...perhaps the next fifty years—you decide. I have an important date to keep.' He looked at his father. 'You can talk to me about your grief any time, but don't ever try to bully me with it.'

He turned and walked out, and there stood Jasmine, with her husband who loved her; and he had never felt more of a bastard than now, as he saw her standing there.

Except she wasn't crying, and he had not lied. She was so much stronger now.

'You told them?' she asked.

He heard the quaver in her voice, but she smiled.

'I did.'

'Well done.'

Julius had not known he could produce tears. Not even when his brother had died had he produced them. He had sat quietly, silently, as Tobias had informed him of the awful news. But his eyes stung now.

'I went back on my word...' he said.

'No.' Jasmine shook her head. 'What if the woman you fall in love with can't have children? The threat will always be there for me, and now it's being dealt with. I have my husband, and I have my daughter.' She looked at him. 'And I have a brother who stands up for what is right.'

She looked up as her mother came out.

'Jasmine...'

'I can't stay, Mama,' Jasmine said. 'Arabella is waiting to tell me about puppy school.'

'Julius,' his father said, 'come back inside. We have a closed room. We can properly discuss—'

'I've been trying to do that for a year.'

Beatrice was right; his father was grieving. How could Beatrice, a woman who didn't have any family of her own, know more about families than someone who did?

Perhaps you did have to step back to see what was right before your eyes?

'I really can't,' Julius said. 'I have plans. I have to get home.'

The terrace looked over the lake. The night air was just a little cool and Beatrice stood there, still wrapped in a towel, unable to take in all that had occurred.

She heard the door open behind her and turned to see

that it was Julius. She quickly wiped her cheeks with her hands.

'Thank you for the martinis.'

'Did you like them?'

'A bit sickly, if I'm honest,'

Beatrice didn't want to hear what had happened with his father, nor bear to hear about his future bride. There was something she had to tell him. Two things!

'I looked up that hotel and it is Dante's.'

'You mean, I was right?' Julius said as he tossed his cap onto a table and unclipped all the straps and belts of his uniform and removed the sword.

'You were. And while I was looking up the hotel I saw a wedding photo. It turns out he and Alicia got married. I called her.'

'How did that go?' he asked, oh-so-casually, and yet he could feel his heart thumping as he unbuttoned his jacket, and he understood now her hesitation and her terror.

Had she been dismissed...let down...forgotten...?

'When I returned to Trebordi at nineteen, Alicia had already gone to Milan to look for me. She struggled with her reading and writing and got nowhere...recently she approached Dante to help her and they hired people to search...'

'You're a missing person?'

'Sort of.' She nodded. 'Well, almost...' She took out her phone. 'They thought they might have found me once. A detective sent Alicia this.'

She handed him the phone she was holding and he looked at the photo that Alicia had just sent. It was of Beatrice in her straw hat, with huge dark glasses on.

'That was on my birthday a few weeks ago,' Beatrice

explained. 'They had a detective watching the convent. He had just given them the details of the hire car I used that day when I called…' She was still shaky. 'I didn't have much luck getting through, at first, saying I was an old friend, but then I called back—rather like Jordan does when she's making a reservation for you.'

'Did it work?'

'They put me through to Dante. He was cross with me at first, but then Alicia came to the phone. It was difficult for five minutes—like agony. Alicia was hurt that I'd changed my name. Very hurt.'

'She understood why when you explained, though?'

'We got past that…' Beatrice evaded answering directly. 'It was like we were children again. I mean, we just fell back into our friendship; she's still the Alicia I knew and—'

'You didn't tell her about your mother?'

'I didn't have to. She forgave me. She understood I was hurt and upset.' Beatrice could see his eyes were trying to reach hers and she gave in and met them. 'No, I didn't tell her. I don't think it's a conversation to be had over the phone. It's…'

'Delicate?'

She nodded, knowing and also admitting she had dared to open the door and had shown him the vulnerable, fragile part of her that she guarded so fiercely.

'So you have your twin back?'

'I do.'

'I'm so happy for you,' he told her. 'When will you see her? After Regalsi?'

'About that…'

She was so shy, like a tiny wild bird, and yet she came to him as though she were tame.

'I've been thinking about Regalsi...'

'Have you?'

'I've misjudged things...' She fixed him with her eyes. 'I want a year.'

'Sorry?'

'I want a year without your wedding hanging over us.'

'So what happened to a few days of fun? A week?'

'Well, I've decided that I'd like to have a lot of fun in what's left of my twenties. I'd like to get to thirty and then...' She looked at him. 'I'll be discreet, but I'm not hiding, and I won't be a secret.'

'Your twin's been whispering in your ear.'

Beatrice smiled a new smile. 'Actually, I did most of the talking...'

Gosh, to share her heart with someone who knew her, who cared, must have been so precious, he thought.

'She agrees with you. She thinks I should have fun, let go, loosen up...'

'It's not you, though.'

'No.'

'And even a year's not going to work, is it?'

'No.'

Now she was starting to cry, and he couldn't bear it.

'But I want to try...'

'Will you marry me?'

Her heart stopped. 'You can't marry me...'

'Actually, I just put all my titles into abeyance. I can do whatever the hell I want.'

'Julius!' She felt a deep-seated panic and moved to stand up, but he stopped her. 'What about Jasmine—?'

'She'll be fine. It might not come to it, but I have told my father...' He took a breath. 'You're right. I think my mother is crazy with grief. But whatever happens I'm going to marry the woman I love—if she will have me.'

'You love me?'

'I'm lovesick. Tobias told me so.'

'You've told Tobias? When?'

'This afternoon.'

'And Jordan?'

'Just now.'

'Before you told me?'

'Well, if you turn me down, they're going to need to know why I'm crying at my desk, clutching a jewelled peacock…'

He made her smile, as always. He chose to make her smile as he dealt with the scary things.

'Julius! You can't turn your back on duty.'

'My first duty is to you,' he told her. 'I mean it.'

She thought he had never looked more serious.

'They're passing up a brilliant king, but that's on them. I'm not turning my back, and I will be a better king with you by my side. That's it. So, do I have to ask again? I don't know how this romantic stuff works… Do you want to marry me?'

Then he put a hand over her mouth.

'Before you respond, you should know that there is still a very good chance you would be Queen Consort. Would you want to be?'

He removed his hand.

'I want whatever makes us work.'

'I think we can handle it either way.'

'I would love to marry you, Julius.'

'Good,' he said. 'What else? Do we go and sign something…?'

'No.' She smiled. 'That's it. We have a verbal agreement. Well, there is one more thing... You have to return my peacock...'

'No, he's mine now. And he will sit on my desk. Don't ever say no to me unless you mean it. Or yes...'

'Oh, I mean it. Yes!'

He kissed her with heartfelt emotion, and she kissed him back with the same. Then he removed the towel she'd stopped clutching with ease, and discarded it, and she wrapped her arms around his neck and breathed in his love.

She closed her eyes but could not stop the tears falling. 'I'm happy...' she said.

'I know...'

He was everything she hadn't known she wanted, and just impossible not to completely love...

'Take my boots off,' he told her.

'I can't.'

She couldn't remove herself from him, or stop kissing him.

'Stay there, then...'

He told her that his military wear wasn't designed for easy access, but she didn't care. She was kissing his neck, and his ear, and pressing herself into him.

She hadn't known that she could love so very much. Every part of her, even her heart, felt as if it were opening, and she was wet and ready as he slid into her.

'Oh...' He closed his eyes and told her how good she felt.

'And you...'

He made her unashamed. He lay back and watched her and Beatrice thought she might die with the pleasure that was building—and this time she wasn't fighting it.

All her reservations were left at the door, and she was relaxed as he played with her breasts and then held her hips as he thrust into her, and even as she closed her eyes she knew he was watching her climax.

It shuddered through her, and she felt the swell and rush of him inside her. She was giddy with deep pleasure, and so breathless…looking down at herself, and him, and watching the last beats of their union.

'I love you so much,' she told him.

'I know.'

There was a buzzer pinging over the door. 'That's the serious one,' he told her. 'The King-is-dead one.'

'Should you answer it?'

'No.'

'So we just hide here till they decide?'

'We're not hiding,' he told her. 'Tonight, at least, we're just Julius and Beatrice. We have at least one night of freedom—possibly many more. But for now no rules or protocols apply. So, what do you want to do?'

'I didn't come with a wardrobe…'

'Jordan's sorting that out for you. We can go out or stay in—you choose.'

'Are we escaping by the tunnel?'

'No. I told you—we're not hiding. It can be like a first date.'

'It actually is my first date,' Beatrice said as she looked at him. 'And I don't know what I want to do.'

'Go and have a shower, then get off to the hetaera's dressing room…' He nudged her with his head. 'You can play dress-up.'

It was a very quick shower, and she came out dripping.

'Put on a towel,' he told her. 'Jordan's waiting.'

'Oh, my God!'

'What? Would you rather wear your grey dress again?'

'No.'

She went through a door and down a rather long corridor and into the hetaera's dressing room. And finally she found velvet. Deep red velvet walls and everything wicked—except for Jordan, who smiled.

'I'm so happy…'

'And me.' Beatrice grinned and gave his very loyal PA a hug. 'I don't know what to wear. What do you wear for your first ever date? I don't know where he's taking me.'

'I do.'

And apparently it required a black dress that scooped a little low at the front and far too low at the back, black stockings, and Cuban-heeled dance shoes.

Jordan put loads of liquid black eyeliner on her as Beatrice's hand was shaking too much.

'Is red lipstick over the top?' Beatrice asked.

'Loads of red lipstick.'

A silent palace staff stood reeling as the maverick Prince and his Cuban-heeled date made their way across the passageway and down the central stairs.

'Your Highness…' Phillipe was almost running. 'The King wishes to—'

'Tomorrow,' Julius said, and he knew from Phillipe's sudden reverence and use of his title that the decision had been made.

He would be King.

He just didn't need to hear it tonight.

Tonight was time for a bar on the water's edge, with music so loud there was no chance to speak.

'What would you like to drink?' He had to shout to be heard over the heavy beat of the music.

'Whisky!' Beatrice said. It felt like a whisky kind of night.

'Right…' He took her onto the dance floor, pulled her in close. 'One-two-three…five-six-seven. Remember that.'

'What about four?'

He pulled her tighter in. 'We move direction.'

'Oh.'

'Got it?'

'No.'

It was brilliant to learn, though, and indecent to be joined at the groin, with his hand on her lower back, while she tried to count in her head.

She was dreadful, and nobody cared; they were too busy keeping count themselves. She could feel the music rippling through her, and his kisses were rough and frequent. The bar was a bit shabby and crowded, and not really a great first date location…unless you knew where the night was headed.

And they did.

But right now it was time to dance.

CHAPTER FIFTEEN

'WERE YOU NERVOUS?' Beatrice asked her bridesmaid.

'No,' Alicia said. 'But then, I wasn't marrying a future king.'

'Were you?' Beatrice asked her little flower girl's mother.

'I was so scared I almost had to be sedated,' Jasmine admitted. 'It was the best thing I ever did, though. How are you feeling, Beatrice?'

'Very sure and very scared.'

It was a serious royal wedding, and her dress was both heavy and heavenly, in rich silk the colour of weak tea. It looked dreadful hanging up, but came alive when she slipped it on.

There was no veil, because she didn't want one, and the bouquet was all white flowers, picked that morning by the lake, with one violet so dark it was nearly black— for Claude, whom she wished could stand at his brother's side this day.

Jasmine's husband wanted to stay in the background, but he was an emergency fill-in—just in case—as Julius had chosen Tobias, his very loyal aide, whose baby was due any second.

As Miss Arabella the flower girl went for one more wee, the two sisters of the heart stood alone together.

'Alicia!' Beatrice warned, because her friend was holding a gorgeous clock she had pilfered from the mantelpiece and her open handbag.

'I want a memento,' Alicia teased.

'I have one for you.'

It was a framed copy of a photo—the only one Beatrice had from their childhood—and Alicia had never seen it, nor any others like it.

'You have a photo…' Alicia opened up the present and they looked at the two little girls on the grass, surrounded by nuns. 'Beatrice!' Alicia gasped. 'You cut her out.'

'I did.'

Beatrice had told Alicia who her mother was and they were closer than ever now.

Yes, she *had* chosen her surname with care that day, and she thought back to Julius on the bench, probing, knowing a little and wanting to know more about Beatrice Taylor.

I cut. I separate.

A necessary requirement at times in order to grow.

'Are *you* going to tell *me* something, Alicia?' She looked down at her friend's little bump.

'It's your day today.'

'And this makes it even happier. A baby!'

'Yes.' Alicia beamed. 'You are going to be an aunty, but right now…'

Today Beatrice and Julius became family.

'Bridesmaids!'

Jordan was at the door to the suite, calling for the bridesmaids and in full royal wedding mode, but a wonderful friend too.

And giving Beatrice away was the rather wild boy she'd warned Alicia about—proof that sometimes she got things wrong.

But this was so right.

The crowds were a blur, and the golden dome of the church was shining as if to rival the sun, but it all fell away when she saw his smile.

Julius was in full military uniform. Clean-shaven, he looked younger than the man she had first met.

She was a *very* composed bride. A little cold, some might say. A little too calm for such a big occasion.

But it was easy to be calm, for it was the surest walk of her life.

'Good morning, Beatrice,' he said, when she finally made it down the long aisle.

'Good morning, Julius.'

Such beautiful words to be greeted with each and every day. In bed…via text…however they were delivered, they would always greet the day that way.

Julius closed his eyes briefly as the King loudly blew his nose. He knew his father would miss his other son always, and was relieved that he was a little more able to show that now.

The bride was not misty-eyed.

Beatrice turned and handed her flowers to Alicia, smiling at her very dear friend. 'Thank you,' she said, and she smiled too at Arabella, who was behaving beautifully.

Then she turned to the man who had found her hidden heart.

The service commenced and Beatrice was deeply serious, listening intently and nodding as she heard his vows.

His beautiful voice brought a gentle calm to her soul as he told her, 'I shall love you all the days of my life.'

And she knew those days would start with a month on Regalsi…

* * * * *

WE HOPE YOU ENJOYED
THIS BOOK FROM
HARLEQUIN
PRESENTS

Escape to exotic locations where passion knows no bounds.

Welcome to the glamorous lives of royals and billionaires, where passion knows no bounds. Be swept into a world of luxury, wealth and exotic locations.

8 NEW BOOKS AVAILABLE EVERY MONTH!

#4041 THE KING'S CHRISTMAS HEIR
The Stefanos Legacy
by Lynne Graham
When Lara rescued Gaetano from a blizzard, she never imagined she'd say "I do" to the man with no memory. Or, when the revelation that he's actually a future king rips their passionate marriage apart, that she'd be expecting a precious secret!

#4042 CINDERELLA'S SECRET BABY
Four Weddings and a Baby
by Dani Collins
Innocent Amelia's encounter with Hunter was unforgettable... and had life-changing consequences! After learning Hunter was engaged, she vowed to raise their daughter alone. But now, Amelia's secret is suddenly, scandalously exposed!

#4043 CLAIMED BY HER GREEK BOSS
by Kim Lawrence
Playboy CEO Ezio will do anything to save the deal of a lifetime. Even persuade his prim personal assistant, Matilda, to take a six-month assignment in Greece...as his convenient bride!

#4044 PREGNANT INNOCENT BEHIND THE VEIL
Scandalous Royal Weddings
by Michelle Smart
Her whole life, Princess Alessia has put the royal family first, until the night she let her desire for Gabriel reign supreme. Now she's pregnant! And to avoid a scandal, that duty demands a hasty royal wedding...

HPCNMRA0822

#4045 THEIR DESERT NIGHT OF SCANDAL
Brothers of the Desert
by Maya Blake

Twenty-four hours in the desert with Sheikh Tahir is more than Lauren bargained for when she came to ask for his help. Yet their inescapable intimacy empowers Lauren to lay bare the scandalous truth of their shared past—and her still-burning desire for Tahir...

#4046 AWAKENED BY THE WILD BILLIONAIRE
by Bella Mason

Colliding with a masked stranger at a ball sends shy Emma's pulse skyrocketing. And that's *before* he introduces himself as Alexander Hastings, the CEO with a wild side, which puts him way out of her league! Will Emma step out of the shadows and into the billionaire's penthouse?

#4047 THE MARRIAGE THAT MADE HER QUEEN
Behind the Palace Doors...
by Kali Anthony

To claim her crown, queen-to-be Lise must wed. The man she must turn to is Rafe, the self-made billionaire who once made her believe in love. He'll have to make her believe in it again for passion to be part of their future...

#4048 STRANDED WITH HIS RUNAWAY BRIDE
by Julieanne Howells

Surrendering her power to a man is unacceptable to Princess Violetta. Even *if* that man sets her alight with a single glance! But when Prince Leo tracks his runaway bride down and they are stranded together, he's not the enemy she first thought...

YOU CAN FIND MORE INFORMATION ON UPCOMING HARLEQUIN TITLES, FREE EXCERPTS AND MORE AT HARLEQUIN.COM.

HPCNMRB0822

"Emma," Alex said, pinning her against the wall in a spectacularly graffitied alley, the walls an ever-changing work of art, when he could bear it no more. "I have to tell you. I really don't care about seeing the city. I just want to get you back in my bed."

He could barely believe that he wanted to take her back home. Sending her on her way was the smarter plan. But how smart was it really to deny himself? Emma knew the score. This wasn't about feelings or a relationship. It was just sex.

"Give me the weekend. I promise you won't regret it." His voice was low and rough. He could see in her eyes that she knew just how aroused he was, and with his body against hers, she could feel it.

"I want that too," she breathed.

"What I said before still stands. This doesn't change things."

"I know that." She grinned. "I don't want it to."

Don't miss
Awakened by the Wild Billionaire
available October 2022 wherever
Harlequin Presents books and ebooks are sold.

Harlequin.com

HPEXP0822